Did the past count for nothing?

"You expected me to stay crazy about you for the rest of my life, I suppose?" Zoe snarled. Rory knew she'd been wildly in love with him, but Zoe thought it was safely in the past.

Rory kneeled on the floor beside her, wicked mockery in his face. "Are we going to stop playing games now?" he asked.

"I don't play games!" Zoe began to scramble to her feet, but he was too quick for her. He pushed her backward, pinning her to the carpet, and glared into her darkening eyes.

"Don't you?" His mouth twisted in an incredulous smile. "Come on, Zoe, admit it. We both know you came here to find me."

She stared up at his gray eyes brilliant with excitement, hating him—and desiring him even more.

CHARLOTTE LAMB began to write "because it was one job I could do without having to leave the children." Now writing is her profession. She has had more than forty Harlequin novels published since 1978. "I love to write," she explains, "and it comes very easily to me." She and her family live in a beautiful old home on the Isle of Man, between England and Ireland. Charlotte spends eight hours a day working at her typewriter—and enjoys every minute of it.

Books by Charlotte Lamb

HARLEQUIN PRESENTS
842—WHO'S BEEN SLEEPING IN MY BED?
851—SLEEPING DESIRE
874—THE BRIDE SAID NO
898—EXPLOSIVE MEETING
971—HEAT OF THE NIGHT
987—LOVE IN THE DARK
1001—HIDE AND SEEK
1025—CIRCLE OF FATE
1042—KISS OF FIRE
1059—WHIRLWIND

HARLEQUIN ROMANCE
2696—KINGFISHER MORNING
2804—THE HERON QUEST

CHARLOTTE LAMB

echo of passion

Harlequin Books

TORONTO • NEW YORK • LONDON
AMSTERDAM • PARIS • SYDNEY • HAMBURG
STOCKHOLM • ATHENS • TOKYO • MILAN

Harlequin Presents first edition June 1988
ISBN 0-373-11081-2

Original hardcover edition published in 1987
by Mills & Boon Limited

CHAPTER ONE

ZOE would never have seen the portrait of herself in the bath if she hadn't noticed an advertisement for the exhibition while she was casually flicking through the pages of an arts magazine at the dentist. She was in the waiting-room, eager to get through her usual six-monthly check-up and with only half a mind on what she was looking at. When the name of the artist leapt out at her she was already turning the page and hurriedly flicked back to find the advertisement, the colour ebbing from her face.

'Miss Stroud? Mr Sheldon will see you now,' the receptionist said a second later, fixing her with a bright, encouraging smile as Zoe dazedly looked up.

'Sorry?' Zoe muttered, and the receptionist's smile automatically became even more soothing.

'Mr Sheldon's ready for you, Miss Stroud. Nothing to worry about, just a routine check.'

Zoe had thrown down the copy of the magazine and followed her into the surgery, but although she didn't go back afterwards to look up the name of the gallery or check the date of the exhibition, her unconscious must have registered both indelibly, because the next day she found herself walking down Bond Street and into the narrow alley which housed the art gallery. She told herself that she was looking for pale blue shoes to wear with a cream linen dress she had just bought, and when she halted outside the gallery she tried to pretend to be surprised to see it, but she didn't do a very good job of fooling herself.

If Rory Ormond had been in sight, she wouldn't have gone in, but as she stared through the plate-glass windows she saw no sign of him. Once she was certain it was safe, she followed a party of ladies in flowery hats into the first room and bought a catalogue which didn't tell her anything she didn't know about the artist. The cover carried a self-portrait that made her neck beat with a savage pulse. It had been painted since she last saw him; he looked different, harder, more angles to his profile, his hair blacker, his eyes more piercing.

She got a sudden feeling that he had painted the picture with anger; it was self-accusing, no excuses made. The artist didn't like himself much.

She looked for it among the landscapes and small still-lifes; Rory had a very distinct style now, he had begun to paint with real force and power, Zoe was impressed, and so, she gathered, were most of the other people in the room. She deliberately eavesdropped on their murmured talk, as interested as if they talked of her.

It was when she walked into an inner room that she saw the pictures of herself and stopped dead, swallowing in shock. She had forgotten that he had painted her—or rather, the memory had been overlaid with more painful memories. The portrait of Rory hung among them, flanked on each side by them, and people stood in front of them all, chattering.

'Wonderful skin tones, look at the shadow on the breasts, that arm over her head, those little blue veins.'

'He's abandoned portraits lately, I wonder why—these

are so good. The old brass taps on that bath are so solid you feel you could turn them and water would gush out.'

'Ralph, come and see this little sketch of the girl's head! Just a few lines, but he's really got it all.'

Zoe's eyes were fixed on the face she remembered but no longer saw in the mirror every morning. Her hair had been long, then; it poured down over her shoulder in a shining black waterfall almost reaching her waist. He had arranged it the way he wanted it; spending minutes settling a strand this way, another that, stroking and fondling it to make it lie exactly in the right position. She shivered, remembering the cool brush of his fingertips on her skin; on her naked breasts, her throat, her cheek. She had hardly dared to breathe. When he was working he was ruthless and inexorable. He glared blackly at her if she begged to be allowed a break and she would sit there in the slowly chilling water, shivering, skin goose-pimpled, body aching, praying that he would get tired and let her stop posing.

Was I really that young? she wondered as she stared at the small, oval face, pale-skinned and vulnerable, with those wide blue eyes and the mouth he insisted must be innocent of lipstick.

'Get that make-up off!' he had snapped the first time she sat for him. 'You don't need that stuff! You'll ruin your lovely skin.'

She had glowed with delight in the compliment and the memory made her angry now. She had been ridiculously young, even for seventeen; you could see it in that big-eyed gaze out of the canvases—a helpless, ecstatic abandonment to his will. You didn't need to be an art critic to read the expression on that girl's face; she blushed as she stared at it and couldn't bear to look any more.

Turning to hurry away, she cannoned into someone standing behind her. The room was crowded, people pushed and wriggled to get a better view. Muttering an automatic apology, Zoe glanced at the stranger. 'Sorry!'

'Okay,' he said, giving her an equally brief glance, then he did a double-take, his jaw dropping.

Zoe pushed her way out of the gallery and began to walk quickly down the alley back into Bond Street; almost bewildered to find herself in a busy London road again. Her mind was trapped seven years back in another place, another time. She had been another person, too, she thought, turning the corner.

It was then that she realised she was being followed. Out of the corner of her eye she saw a tweed jacket, recognised it and felt her mouth go dry. It was the man from the art gallery! He had followed her out and was treading on her heels. Zoe began to walk much faster, almost running, and felt him hurrying too to keep up with her.

She was no longer the shy, inexperienced innocent, Rory had painted—glancing sideways as she passed a shop window she saw a fleeting reflection of a very sophisticated young woman in a chic red dress and sighed with relief. Surely nobody could have recognised her from the paintings in the gallery? Seven years was a long time and she looked completely different.

She paused to look into a shop window, pretending to stare at some hats while she actually studied the man following her. He had halted at her side, quite openly, and as she was about to turn away he cleared his throat and Zoe looked round at him.

'Excuse me!' he said, rather flushed, and she lifted one cold eyebrow.

'Yes?' He tried a smile and she considered it without smiling back.

'I saw you in Walbury's gallery just now,' he mumbled.

'Really?' She tapped one pointed toe in an expensive, delicate Italian-made black shoe, and he looked down at it nervously.

'I'm sure I recognised . . .' He was stammering, his ears red. 'Those are pictures of you, aren't they? Ormond did paint you?'

Zoe's frozen calm deserted her at that moment; she could not bear to talk about Rory, she was appalled by the thought of this stranger staring at her and remembering the images of her naked body in the bath. She felt shamed, as if discovered naked in the street.

An empty taxi cruised past and she began to run after it, waving an arm. The driver pulled up and she tumbled into the back, panting out her address. It was extravagant to take a taxi all the way to St John's Wood, but this was an emergency, she felt.

Her pursuer skidded to a halt on the kerb just as the taxi moved away again. Zoe glanced round, breathing thickly. The man's brown eyes gazed after her; their expression a mixture of frustration, impatience and something she suddenly felt was unhappiness. He had an open, fair-skinned face, very English; rugged and healthy, his nose long and firm, his jaw obstinate and his mouth well-cut. He didn't look the type to pursue girls in the street; she couldn't believe he needed to, he was probably more often pursued himself. He was casually but expensively dressed in a good tweed jacket and grey trousers. He looked nice, and Zoe settled back into the corner of her taxi wondering why he *had* followed her. He couldn't be a reporter, could he?

When she got to her flat she found Fiona in for once, such a rare occurrence that Zoe stared incredulously. 'Good lord, hello! Fancy meeting you here!' she said, and her flatmate grimaced hideously.

Fiona was wearing a Japanese kimono lavishly embroidered with a red and gold dragon. She had piled her blonde hair on top of her head and skewered it with a gilded comb. Staring at her, Zoe at once suspected they were about to have a visitor. Fiona was dressed to kill, and that meant she expected a man.

'I hate your idea of sarcasm!' said Fiona, setting out little bowls of something pink in clear aspic.

'Shrimps?' asked Zoe, reaching for one, and Fiona slapped her hand.

'I'm entertaining for lunch. He should be here any minute. Make yourself scarce, will you, there's a pal.'

The doorbell rang; Fiona threw a hurried glance at her own reflection in a mirror near the door which she had carefully hung there when she moved into Zoe's flat a year ago. 'Always have a mirror by the door,' she explained. 'That gives you a chance to take that last look before he sees you.'

Zoe had laughed and Fiona had stared reprovingly. She took conquest very seriously. She had an image of sexual relationships as a war-game in which she meant to be the winner; the outcome of the final battle marriage, of course. So far she hadn't met the man she was waiting for, but she enjoyed the skirmishing.

Disappearing into her own bedroom, Zoe closed the door. She was well trained. Looking at her watch, she decided to go out for lunch at the nearby bistro. It was sometimes crowded on a Saturday, but it was early enough for her to manage to get a table if she hurried.

She heard voices as she ran a comb through her short, layered black hair. Her make-up was still immaculate, but she saw a flush lingering in her face, and turned away so that she need not start thinking about Rory Ormond again.

Fiona opened the door and came in and Zoe turned ruefully. 'Okay, I'm just going!'

'It wasn't him, it was for you,' said Fiona, looking curious.

'For me? Who is it?'

'I didn't ask, but he's dishy.' Fiona had an acquisitive gleam that Zoe recognised as the look she wore whenever she saw an attractive man—not that she ever poached, but Zoe always knew when Fiona rather fancied the man someone else had in tow.

Puzzled, Zoe was about to walk into their sitting-room when a premonition struck her and she froze. 'Is he fair?' she asked, and Fiona nodded. 'Wearing a tweed jacket? Grey pants?' Fiona looked amused as she agreed.

Zoe sat down on the bed. 'Oh, no! How did he find me?'

'What's this all about?' asked Fiona, bright-eyed and fascinated.

'Tell him I'm out!'

'I can hardly do that. I just told him you were in! He's new, isn't he? Had a row? He looks much too nice to quarrel with, Zoe—give him another chance, whatever he's done!'

'I don't even know him!' Zoe protested irritably, and Fiona stared even more.

'Then how did you know what he looked like? You're crazy, what on earth do you mean? Have you only just met? Why don't you want to talk to him?'

'I wish I knew how he'd manged to track me down,' Zoe thought aloud. 'He didn't even know my name!'

The doorbell went again and Fiona said impatiently, 'Well, whatever happens you aren't ruining my lunch-party. Mark's special and I've been planning this for two days. I've gone to a lot of trouble to make a Japanese meal because Mark loves Japanese food, and you aren't spoiling it, Zoe. Take this guy for a walk, make him buy you lunch, but get him off the premises!'

She pushed Zoe reluctantly towards the door as the doorbell buzzed again. As they both went into the sitting-room they heard male voices; one of them distinctly displeased. The fair young man had opened the front door and Fiona's latest boy-friend was bristling as he walked past him.

'Mark darling,' Fiona purred hurriedly, fluttering towards him with tiny little steps to put both full-sleeved arms around his neck to kiss him.

He allowed her kiss, then pulled back his head and eyed her accusingly. 'I thought this was a lunch for two? Who's he?'

'Zoe and . . . sorry, what did you say your name was?' Fiona turned to smile at the fair man.

'Oliver,' he said. 'Oliver Naughton.'

'Oliver's taking Zoe out for lunch, darling,' Fiona told

Mark Shelby, whose frown smoothed out. He was a city man, a stockbroker with international business connections. Zoe found him a little bullish, aggressively masculine and without much conversation, but at the moment Fiona was apparently enjoying playing up to him. Zoe hoped the affair wouldn't last long. Luckily, Fiona's flights of romance never did. She wouldn't allow them to get boring. Once she had decided a man wasn't what she was looking for Fiona magically disposed of him. Zoe often wondered how she did it without apparent trouble; Fiona had a flair for diplomacy. Indeed, that was her job—despite her glamorous appearance and love of social life Fiona was a highly qualified civil servant with the Foreign Office. Two years older than Zoe, she had an impressive degree and passed examinations with cool ease.

Mark Shelby smiled politely at Zoe. 'How are you, Zoe? You look charming, that shade of red suits you.'

She managed to smile back, carefully avoiding the fair man's watching eyes. Her mind was working overtime, trying to think of a way of getting rid of him.

'I'm fine. How's the Stock Market? Booming?'

'I'm not complaining,' Mark said complacently. 'What about you? Life in the advertising business still good?'

'I enjoy it.'

'Money for old rope!' he teased, and she forced a smile.

'If you say so.' She and Mark had this conversation every time they met. Small talk appeared to be his only idea of communication; once he had exhausted that he lapsed into silence, talked about the weather or began a tedious anecdote about golf or his latest coup on the Stock Exchange.

He looked at his watch. 'Well . . .'

Fiona said quickly, 'Zoe, you and Oliver don't want to be too late to get a table!'

Drowningly, Zoe at last met the fair man's eyes and he gave her a pleading little smile. She saw she had no option and walked towards the door with him hurrying to open it for her.

'See you later,' Fiona called sweetly. Zoe heard the unspoken addition; much later, thank you! Don't hurry back! She threw Fiona a dry look as she walked out of the flat, and Fiona winked.

'I'm sorry,' said Oliver Naughton as they walked out into the street. 'I had to talk to you.'

'How did you find me?' That, at least, she had to know!

'Got the next taxi and gave him the address I'd heard you give your driver.'

She made a face. 'Oh, I see.' It had been simpler than she had imagined; he hadn't needed magic powers, just good hearing.

He paused on the pavement, looking down at her. 'Anywhere special you'd like to eat?'

'There's no need for you to buy me lunch.' She confronted him, her chin up and her blue eyes cool. 'What exactly do you want, Mr Naughton?'

'Oliver, please. I want to talk to you about Rory Ormond.'

She knew that already, and he hadn't really answered her question. 'What about him? I haven't seen him for years.' Her eyes narrow, she added, 'Are you a journalist?'

'Good lord, no!' He looked almost insulted. 'I'm a

farmer, a sheep-farmer.'

She smiled because he said it with such satisfaction and he looked the part; his skin had an open-air flush and he had clear, healthy brown eyes.

'But why are you so interested in Rory Ormond?' she asked, a puzzled frown pulling her brows together.

He looked at her uneasily, angrily, uncertainly. 'I have a cousin, Lindy. She's eighteen and she's lost her head over Ormond. She won't listen to me and I'm scared for her. I don't trust him, he'll hurt her, I'm sure of it.' He stared insistently and Zoe felt herself flushing. 'Won't he?' he added, and she wondered how much he had read into those paintings of her, how much had Rory Ormond painted into her face, into her wide, adoring eyes?

'What makes you think I can tell you?' she asked defensively, because she saw no reason for confiding in a stranger.

His mouth turned down. 'There was something in your face when I spoke to you.' He looked hopeless, but he wasn't giving up just yet. 'Look, let me take you to lunch. I'm quite safe, honestly.'

Zoe eyed his face with sudden amusement. He didn't need to tell her she could trust him; it was written there for all the world to see, and if she hadn't been in such a state of disturbed confusion when he had followed her in the street she wouldn't have run away from him in the first place.

'There's a bistro round the corner. The food's good and the prices aren't going to bankrupt you. If you like French cooking.'

'I like any food,' he said cheerfully and with frankness, then paused. 'Except Japanese,' he added more cautiously. 'Your friend gave me a piece of raw fish. I ate it, but I prefer my fish cooked.'

Zoe laughed. 'So do I.' She had a suspicion Fiona preferred it cooked, too; another reason why the affair with Mark wouldn't last much longer.

'We can walk to the bistro,' she told him, and they set off at a casual pace. It was getting hotter, and Oliver Naughton took off his tweed jacket and carried it over his arm; he looked flushed.

'This isn't a formal sort of place, is it?' he asked, eyeing Zoe sideways. 'You look very elegant, but my old tweeds aren't really London standard, are they? And I'm not wearing a tie.'

'Oh, they won't mind,' she assured him, but he looked a lot easier once he had seen the motley collection of people lunching at the bistro. They were given a table in a corner and a handwritten menu which was also chalked up on a blackboard on the wall. They both chose a fruit cocktail to start with and then the navarin of lamb which was one of the house specialities. Zoe assured him it was always tender and had a delicious flavour; the vegetables were fresh and well cooked.

'Can we have a bottle of wine right away?' Oliver asked the waiter, picking a rosé wine from the extensive list, and it wasn't until they were sipping the first glass that he asked her, 'When did you meet Ormond?'

'Seven years ago, in Provence.' She looked down at the pink wine, one fingertip rubbing the chilled glass, her mouth wry. 'Did you know that every seven years every one of your body cells dies and is replaced? That means that I'm a completely different person from the girl he painted.' Physically, anyway, she thought. Did it apply to your brain cells too? 'I'm surprised you recognised me!' she added lightly, and felt Oliver staring.

'You've changed a lot,' he agreed. 'Your hair's been cut off, you're very different in some ways, all the same I knew you at once.' His mouth tightened angrily. 'He's a brilliant painter, damn him!'

'That was obvious, even seven years ago!' said Zoe. 'I didn't know anything about art, although I thought I did. I thought I knew everything.'

'So does Lindy.' Oliver drank some wine hurriedly, as though he needed it, had to have the quick injection of fire it gave. 'She's so blind with infatuation she can't see him clearly. I'd like to kill him!'

His fury was rather too personal to be that of a cousin, however fond, and Zoe gave him a searching look. How old was he? In his late twenties? He was obviously in love with his cousin. She felt a sting of curiosity about the other girl—what did she look like? Was she fair, like Oliver?

'You must have been her age when he painted you,' Oliver said morosely. 'He's painting her, over and over again. She's just left school, she's just a kid, the swine!'

'I was seventeen. I was working at a hotel in Provence during my school holidays to improve my French because I was taking it for my final exams the following year. It was hard work, it was a small family hotel and they expected you to be up at first light and kept you busy until very late. In the mornings I made beds and laid tables, then I had the afternoons off from two o'clock until seven. In the evenings I waited at table and then helped to wash up before I finally got to bed. It was exhausting, but once I'd met him I spent all my free time with him. He painted me every afternoon. I had Sundays off and sometimes he would paint me all day. I loved it.'

She had been talking in a low, husky voice, her head bent and her eyes on the wine in her glass. She was remembering and found the process painful. She had been so in love, and she hated the man who had used her ruthlessly and then walked away without a backward look.

'Was he living in France then?' Oliver asked, and she nodded.

'He had a little villa he was renting from a friend.' It had been secluded, peaceful, a simple, white-walled building behind stone walls with a garden full of cypress and olive-trees and tiny lizards. They had often eaten out there; picnic meals of salad and fruit and cheese. If she closed her eyes she could hear the whirr of the cicadas and smell the pine resin.

'He's got a house in Scarlett on the cliffs,' said Oliver, and she looked at him quickly.

'Scarlett? Where's that?'

'Cumbria, a few miles up the coast from Whitehaven,' he told her, surprising her. She hadn't been expecting that answer; it was so far away.

'Do *you* live there?'

He nodded. 'I farm a place my family have owned for three generations, our land runs from the outskirts of the village up into the hills. It's mainly rough grazing, but it suits sheep.'

'And Lindy?'

'She still lives with her father—her mother's dead and she's an only child. She's spoilt, I suppose. George dotes on her. You can't blame him, she's a darling and she's all he's got.'

'What does he think about Rory Ormond?' Zoe asked, and saw him frown heavily. The waiter appeared with their first course and there was a moment's pause before Oliver answered her.

Lifting a spoonful of orange and melon delicately sprinkled with chopped mint, he eyed it distastefully as he said, 'George teaches art at our nearest comprehensive. He thinks Rory Ormond's a genius and he's as flattered as hell to have Lindy painted by the great man. George thinks she's being immortalised, he worships every brush stroke. When I told him I thought the man was a rat and a fink he looked at me as if I was crazy and laughed.' Oliver turned a slow, dark red. 'He hinted that I was just jealous, which is ridiculous. I'm only worried about Lindy.'

'Is George your uncle?' Zoe frowned, trying to work out the relationships.

'Cousin,' said Oliver, looking taken aback. 'My mother was his father's youngest sister, there was twelve years between them and my mother married late in life. George was fourteen when I was born and he got married himself when I was just putting on long trousers.' He saw the muddled expression on Zoe's face and added patiently, 'I'm twenty-eight, he's forty-two. Lindy's seventeen.'

Kindly, Zoe advised, 'Eat your fruit salad, it's delicious.' Watching him, she hoped he wasn't going to bolt the whole meal like that or he would have indigestion afterwards.

While they were waiting for their navarin to arrive,

Oliver murmured tentatively, 'You were in love with him, weren't you?' His ears were pink, she could see he hated having to ask, and that made it easier for her to answer frankly.

'Head over heels, and you're right—he hurt me badly. All that summer I thought it was the real thing and I was in heaven, and then one day he was gone and I never saw him again. It was like falling off the top of a mountain. I didn't think I'd ever hit bottom, and when I did I didn't think I'd ever get over it. In one way it was a good thing. I went back to school and worked like a slave, just to keep my mind off him. I got terrific grades and went to university and did well there. If it hadn't been for Rory Ormond I doubt if I'd have done as well as I did, but at the time I certainly wasn't grateful to him.' She paused as the waiter arrived with their second course.

'I wish you'd tell Lindy all that,' Oliver burst out, and that was when she saw exactly why he had chased her and been so insistent. 'If she knew the sort of guy he is, I'm sure she'd snap out of it.'

Sadly, Zoe shook her head at him. 'Don't count on it. She probably wouldn't believe you, or me, come to that. If she's in love she'll believe what she wants to believe.'

'She's so young! I can't bear to watch,' Oliver said glumly, and attacked his lamb with ferocity, glowering down at it as if he were taking a knife and fork to Rory Ormond.

Over coffee, he suddenly said, 'I suppose you couldn't come up to Scarlett for a few days? My mother's very hospitable and there are several spare bedrooms in the farmhouse, you would enjoy yourself, and I'd be very grateful. I could drive you up, I've got my car here. I had

to come to London on business anyway and I went along
to see Ormond's exhibition because I thought I might
find out something more about him. He's so damn
secretive, he hardly tells you anything about himself.'

'You were hunting for ammunition, were you?' Zoe
asked with amusement, and he looked sheepish.

'Something like that. Meeting you was a stroke of luck
I didn't expect. I knew those paintings of you pretty well
before today—he has them in his studio. He would never
sell them, George says. He's had some fabulous offers.
You know he usually paints landscapes and so the dealers
would love to get their hands on the rare portraits he's
done, but Ormond won't even talk about selling them.'

She looked up, her face blank with a peculiar sense of
shock. 'Oh?' She hoped she sounded casual; she was
feeling very strange. Her head was light, her ears buzzed.
Why wouldn't he sell the portraits of her?

Oliver was watching her like a cat at a mousehole,
eagerness in his eyes. 'Lindy has always been eaten up
with curiosity about you, because of that. If she saw you,
she'd be jealous, I'm sure of it.'

Zoe had turned pale, then flushed. 'You're very
scheming,' she said huskily.

'I'm pretty down-to-earth, normally,' he said. 'It's just
that I don't want to see Lindy getting hurt, and I don't
trust Ormond an inch.'

She considered him drily. 'And how do you propose to
explain to him how I come to be staying with you?'

'Oh,' he said, looking confused, 'I hadn't thought of
that, but does it matter?'

'He's bound to ask, he's bound to be very curious.' Am
I really considering doing this? Zoe asked herself in

disbelief. That would be crazy. I don't even know this girl and she means nothing to me. I'm sorry for Oliver, I like him, but I doubt if anything either he or I could do would bring Lindy to her senses. Rory Ormond cast a potent spell. She remembered that only too well. It wouldn't be easy to disillusion an eighteen-year-old in the grip of wild infatuation, and they couldn't count on co-operation from Rory Ormond. If he guessed what they were up to, he would make sure they didn't succeed. He had a wickedly mischievous streak. He would run rings around someone like Oliver Naughton and get a kick out of tormenting him.

'We could say I met you in London and . . .' Oliver stared fixedly at her, his mind working. 'And . . .'

She waited, half smiling.

'And fell in love,' he ended with a flash of inspiration. 'They couldn't very well argue with that, could they? I mean, I'd say I'd always loved those paintings of you . . .' He broke off, his neck red as he suddenly remembered them, and gulped for air. 'Well, anyway, I don't see that there's a problem. Coincidences do happen. Why shouldn't we meet by accident and decide we like each other?'

'You underestimate Rory Ormond. He'll guess there's more to it than that.'

'Let him! As long as we convince Lindy!' He gave her one of his imploring looks. He was beginning to remind Zoe of a dog she had once had; it had stared at her in just that way when it wanted to be taken for a walk, sitting up, its lead in its mouth, tail wagging.

'Please come,' he pleaded. 'For Lindy's sake!'

'If I come it will be for my own sake,' Zoe told him. 'I'd

enjoy spiking Rory Ormond's guns. It's time somebody did.' She tried to sound lighthearted, but from the way Oliver looked at her, she suspected she sounded grimly vengeful and hurriedly gave him a brilliant smile to cover her tracks.

'Well, why not?' she added. 'I've nothing much on at the moment, and I don't know your part of the world at all. It could be fun.'

'Can you get time off work?'

'I'm a freelance, I can come and go as I please.'

'A freelance what?' Oliver asked curiously.

'Copy-writer. I work for advertising agencies—at the moment I have a contract with one in particular, but my time's my own to arrange and I'm between projects at the moment. When do we go?'

'I'm in London until Friday. I've got to sign some papers at a solicitor's office—a distant relative died and left his house to me and it's being sold. I've had to come down to oversee the arrangements. My parents thought I should. We don't know this solicitor and they thought I ought to check on him on the spot.'

Zoe smiled at this caution but looked down to hide her amusement. 'Very wise, no doubt.'

'You never know,' Oliver said firmly.

'That's true. You never do.'

'I rarely come to London; in fact, this is only the third time I've been here, so I've made a holiday of it. Seen shows, done some shopping, gone sightseeing. Pity to waste the opportunity.'

'Are you staying at a hotel?'

He nodded and told her the name of the hotel, but Zoe didn't know it. 'It's small,' Oliver confessed. 'I wasn't

wasting money on a big hotel. This is fine for me and I
can park my car behind the hotel. It isn't in the centre of
London, but it isn't far away.' He called for the bill, and
after he had paid it with cash they walked out into the
afternoon sunlight and paused on the pavement.

'I could pick you up at your flat,' he offered. 'On
Friday morning early?'

'How early?' she asked cautiously.

'It's a long drive. Would six o'clock be too early for
you?'

Zoe's eyes widened in horror. 'Much too early! I'd be a
zombie at that hour. How about seven?'

Oliver agreed, but when she opened her door to him
the following Friday it was only a quarter to seven and he
was lucky she was fully awake. She would have been
asleep if Fiona hadn't woken her up from a deep sleep by
coming in at six o'clock after an all-night party, and
falling over Zoe's suitcase, which she had placed by the
front door where she could pick it up as she left.

The crash and the language Fiona used afterwards
brought Zoe stumbling out into the hallway, yawning.

'You're really going!' Fiona attacked her at once, dark-
eyed after a night of dancing and talking. 'I didn't believe
you'd do it! You're crazy, Zoe—don't go!'

'I can look after myself, and I owe him one!' said Zoe,
feeling her way along the wall to their bathroom to take a
quick, cold shower.

Fiona followed, convulsively yawning. 'It never works
to try to get your own back on a man! It just shows him
you still care, don't you know that? The best way to get
back at them is ignore them.'

'I'm going to rescue this girl, that's all! I wish someone

had come along and done the same for me seven years ago!'

Fiona laughed cynically. 'Darling, where love's concerned, none of us ever listens to good advice! When you've had the bad luck to meet a guy like that, you chalk it up to experience and concentrate on getting over him as soon as possible.'

'I am over him! And I mean to stay that way! But I want to make sure he doesn't break this girl's heart and walk away. Oliver Naughton's in love with her, it stood out a mile. I'm just going to play fairy godmother to them both. Or do I mean Cupid?'

'Stupid, not Cupid,' said Fiona, giving up the unequal struggle, and staggering off to bed to sleep off her party.

By the time Oliver arrived, Zoe was dressed and waiting for him, and by nine o'clock they were well on their way up north. They stopped for breakfast near Birmingham and by noon they had almost reached the Lake District; Oliver had a fast car and the motorway wasn't too crowded. He drove without talking much, but during the journey Zoe learnt a good deal about him and his family and told him quite a bit about herself in snatches. He was obviously fond of his parents who lived in the farmhouse with him. His father, he said, had arthritis, and couldn't work the way he had any more. He helped on his good days and insisted on doing most of the considerable paperwork even when he wasn't fit enough to work outside. Mrs Naughton cooked and cleaned and looked after the hens and ducks and bottle-fed orphaned lambs or very weak ones which couldn't be left with their mother.

Zoe gained a clear picture of their lives in the isolated

farmhouse and wondered how her own arrival would be met. What would his parents think when their only son brought home a strange female from London?

As Oliver crested a hill and slowed to point out the farmhouse below them in a green valley, Zoe had an attack of nerves.

'Your family are going to be amazed to see me!' she pointed out huskily. 'Don't you think you ought to give them some warning?' She knew Oliver hadn't yet told them he was bringing someone back with him, he had already admitted that.

'A bit late now,' muttered Oliver, rather flushed. She looked sideways and saw that he was frowning anxiously; as much a prey to last-minute nerves as herself.

Zoe looked at the house again, admiring the sturdy lines of it. It was simply designed, reminding her of a child's drawing of a house; thick, whitewashed walls and a blue-grey slate roof, flat, nicely proportioned windows on each side of a heavy oak front door. Outbuildings lay behind it and close to the house grew holly bushes, thorn trees, pine and yew, all bent and contorted in the prevailing wind. This was a wild landscape; on one side you could see the grey-blue distances of the sea and on the other rock and heather and gorse, and the craggy rising of hills which stretched back until they vanished into misty blues and mournful slaty greys.

'Why don't I go for a walk while you drive to the house and talk to your parents?' she suggested. Her stomach was knotted; she wished she hadn't come. Fiona had been right—it was a crazy idea and she had been too impulsive.

Oliver was driving along a narrow, winding road with

stone walls on either side and behind them rough pastures in which sheep grazed. He was looking around on either side with a contented eye now.

'It's good to be home,' he said, and Zoe saw he hadn't been listening to her.

'Oliver, listen! Drop me at your gate and I'll walk up the drive—that will give you time to warn your family I'm on my way!'

He turned and shrugged. 'Okay, but they may think that a bit odd.'

'At least you'll have given them time to get over the first surprise.' And time to say what they might otherwise have said in front of her or politely bitten back in a way which was even worse! For the first time, Zoe considered the question of whether or not Oliver's parents had ever seen those paintings of her in Rory Ormond's studio, and her spirit quailed at the idea. She looked at Oliver, about to ask him, then couldn't bring herself to do so. Better not to know, she decided!

'What on earth shall I say to them?' asked Oliver, his face showing her that he was getting more worried as they grew closer to the moment when he had to tell his parents about her.

They were almost at the wide, green-painted wooden gates and he had slowed to a crawl. 'Stop the car, let me get out,' Zoe said, and he obeyed. She scrambled out into the road and turned back to say, 'I'll give you half an hour, right?'

She didn't wait for him to answer, she crossed the road and began walking over springy grass and heather towards the sea. It was a bright, hot afternoon; there were white-winged gulls with black heads flying around

the cliff on which she was walking, and she watched their
gliding flight with admiration. Gorse-bushes in vivid
yellow bloom, campion and willowherb, gave splashes of
colour to the tussocky grass. Zoe hadn't been to the sea
for some time; she slowed as she came close to the cliff-
edge, staring at the flashing, glittering water. In spite of
the heat, there was a fresh wind blowing and her hair
suddenly whisked across her face. It was through that
fine curtain of hair that she saw Rory Ormond on the
beach below.

He was coming out of the sea; his lean, tanned body
bare except for a pair of black trunks. Drops of water
pearled the black hair on his chest, his broad shoulders
glistened moistly. Dry-mouthed, Zoe stared down. He
hadn't changed at all. He must be in his late thirties now,
yet there wasn't a grey hair among the thick black
strands clinging wetly to his scalp and giving him the
look of a human seal. He had always been tall and thin;
his features chiselled and hard, faintly withdrawn at
times, as though he could move into another world and
forget everything around him. Her eyes searched for
some difference in him and only found a change of
temperament. Rory had laughed a good deal when she
knew him in France. His eyes had mocked, his smile
teased. This man walking up on to the rocky beach
looked as if he rarely smiled; his face was set in saturnine
lines, his straight, tough mouth had power and perhaps
even sensuality in the folds of it, but the laughter and
charm were not visible.

She watched him put up a hand to slick back some wet
hair. At that instant he glanced idly upwards and saw her
on the cliff top. Zoe saw his face tighten, his grey eyes

widen, flash, his long-limbed body tense. Inexplicably she was suddenly panic-stricken. She turned and ran back from the cliff top towards the fields of Oliver's farm. She had walked for a long time and the house was quite distant, but it would take Rory quite a while to climb the steep cliff path she had noticed before she saw him and by the time he reached the top of the cliff she would be safely inside the gates of Oliver's farm.

As she ran she shivered, as if it were deepest winter, not summer. She shouldn't have come. She had made a dangerous mistake.

CHAPTER TWO

SHE was almost at the gate when it happened—she saw a
small red sports car zipping along the road and her head
went back to watch it so that she was no longer looking
where she was going and did not see the rabbit hole in the
heathery grass. Her foot went down into it and she
couldn't save herself. She tumbled forward with a cry of
shock and hit the ground so hard that she couldn't move
for a moment, just lying there with her eyes shut and her
head throbbing from the impact. When she did scramble
to her knees she found the landscape dizzily revolving
and stayed where she was, blinking at it as it slowed
down.

The red sports car had turned into the farm drive; she
saw it vanishing a second before she heard the pad of
running feet on the cliff-top behind her. Her fall had
made her forget Rory Ormond; she was half dazed as she
turned her head to look back over her shoulder. He must
have stopped to dress; he was now wearing charcoal grey
cotton trousers and an open-necked white shirt, but the
shirt clung to his body damply and his black hair was still
wet.

Zoe's eyes flew to his face and met a fixed, searching
stare. 'So it is you!' he said, and she felt her nerves flicker
at the familiarity of that deep, husky voice. 'Zoe, I
thought I was dreaming!'

She felt extremely odd, kneeling there while he loomed

over her, and began to get up. 'Have we met?' she asked
as she did, pretending to look puzzled.

'What do you mean, have we met? You know we
have!' Rory said impatiently, gripping her arms to help
her to her feet.

'Really? I don't remember, I'm afraid.' Zoe tried to
walk away, but he swung her back towards him and took
her chin in one hand, tilting her head so that he could
stare into her face. She recognised that stare; Rory was
observing her the way he did a tree or a flower, purely as
an object. He had a maddening trick of switching from
man to painter in a flash.

'You've changed,' he said, and her mouth indented.
'What did you expect? Don't you think you have?'

'Not this much,' he murmured, and his other hand
gently moved over her features, as if he was a blind man
learning what she looked like by touch. She shivered at
the trail of those cool fingertips over her eye sockets,
nose, cheekbones and mouth. 'What's happened to you?'
he asked her, frowning, and she flared up, angry both
with herself and him because he still had power over her.
She had come here in the confident belief that she could
handle Rory Ormond now; she was an adult, sure of
herself, immunised, safe. She had only been in his
company for five minutes and she was already beginning
to see that she had been over-confident. Rory Ormond
was still capable of casting a potent spell.

'I grew up!' she said, flinging the words at him like
daggers.

His brows curved upwards and he smiled lazily. 'Oh, I
see—you grew up!'

She didn't like the way he smiled and hit out, 'That's

right! I'm not a half-baked kid any more. Seven years is a long time and . . . and will you let go of me?' She pulled her head back sharply and he let go of her chin, his smile mocking now.

'So you do remember me, after all.'

'You just reminded me,' she said, looking away.

'Did you need reminding?'

'A lot has happened since that summer!' She lifted her chin and managed a bright, hard smile.

'Has it?' Rory's eyes had an ominous light that reminded her of the sea on a stormy day with lightning playing over chilly waters. She had wounded his vanity; he preferred to believe himself unforgettable. She felt a little stab of triumph.

He was considering her with his head to one side, and she wished she had put on something more exciting than a crisp white short-sleeved blouse and an elegant dark blue skirt. She had dressed demurely for the benefit of Oliver's parents; she hadn't expected to run into Rory quite so soon.

'Are you married?' he asked abruptly, gripped her wrist and raised her left hand to look at her bare fingers. 'No ring,' he said to himself in a dry way.

'Not yet!' Zoe smiled, injecting into her tone a soft implication that it could happen any day, and Rory let her hand fall back at her side, his face blank. There was a curious silence, then he looked sharply at her, his expression changing.

'What are you doing here?' he demanded, as if he had just thought of it, just realised the strangeness of their meeting like this in the middle of the Cumbrian landscape which was so very different from the hot

Provençal fields in which they had last seen each other.

'I'm staying with someone.' She let her lashes fall again and smiled demurely, feeling him watch her.

'Who?' Rory's head came up as he stared around at the emptiness of sea and sky and rolling fields and hills. 'Where?' he asked, frowning, but just as Zoe was about to answer him they both heard someone walking towards them from the farm. It was Oliver with a couple of sheepdogs at his heels, and as Zoe glanced at him he waved and shouted.

'Coming in for tea?' He was looking eagerly at her and Rory; dying of curiosity at seeing them together, and Zoe hoped he wasn't going to be too obvious, because Rory Ormond had a quick, sharp mind and could put two and two together in a flash. Oliver wasn't very good at hiding his thoughts, either. She made up her mind to talk to him about keeping a tight hold over his expression.

Rory turned his head slowly to stare at her again, his grey glance penetrating, and she saw that she would have to do something quickly to make sure he didn't begin to suspect the conspiracy she and Oliver had hatched.

'I'm staying with Oliver,' she told him hurriedly, and he stared even harder.

'With Oliver?' he repeated, as if he didn't believe his ears. 'I didn't even know you knew him!'

'We met at your exhibition in London,' she began, and he interrupted, his face changing.

'So you went to it!'

Her temper suddenly ran away with her. 'Yes, I did, and I saw those pictures of me—how could you? I didn't know where to look, I was so taken aback! It never even entered my head that you'd show them without asking me first. You had no right to do it!'

'I couldn't ask you, could I? I didn't know where to
find you. I didn't know your home address.'

'Then you shouldn't have put them in the exhibition!'

His eyes flickered oddly and his mouth tightened. 'I
couldn't leave them out. They're some of the best work
I've ever done.'

Zoe took a sharp breath, but couldn't think of anything
to say because she knew that that was probably true. The
paintings had caused the biggest stir at the exhibition;
the crowds around them had been thicker than around
the landscapes and people had seemed full of admiration.
All the same, Zoe hated the thought of all those strangers
staring at her body, and she looked at Rory with hostility.

'I hated seeing them there! I want you to take them out
of the exhibition!'

He frowned blackly at her just as Oliver came up
beside them, and she put out a hand to Oliver, who took
it, his grip firm and comforting.

'Hallo, Ormond!' Oliver said coldly, nodding.

'Enjoy your trip to London?' asked Rory, and Oliver
looked at Zoe again, smiling.

'It was eventful.'

'So I just heard.' Rory's voice was ironic. 'I gather I
had a hand in bringing you two together?'

'That's right. You know I've always admired those
paintings of Zoe, so I recognised her at once. When she
ran out I could see she was upset, so I followed her to see
if I could help and ended up by taking her to lunch. I'd
have liked to stay on in London for a while, getting to
know her better, but I couldn't leave the farm for more
than a few days, so I had to come back. It seemed a good

idea to invite her up here instead.' Oliver's fair-skinned, open face and his calm, even voice were oddly truthful. Zoe didn't see how anyone could doubt a word he said, and was very impressed by his unsuspected ability to act.

Rory turned his head to study her. 'So if I hadn't shown those pictures, you and Naughton might never have met? I'd say you should be grateful to me, not annoyed!'

She bared her teeth. 'I'll try. It won't be easy.' She turned to Oliver. 'We mustn't keep your mother waiting. I'm hungry! Has she made those scones you boasted about?'

'They've just come out of the oven!'

'Oh, goody!' Zoe threw Rory a brief glance. ''Bye!'

Oliver merely nodded to him and neither of them got a reply. Rory stayed where he was, watching them walk away, the dogs running ahead of them now; black and white streaks which vanished along the drive towards the farmhouse. Oliver let out a long, relieved breath.

'Do you think we sold it to him?'

'I hope so.' She didn't sound too sure, and she knew Oliver heard the doubt in her voice by the way he looked quickly at her, frowning. 'How did your parents react when they heard I was here?'

He hesitated, then sighed. 'I'm sure they'll be very nice to you.'

'But?' She knew he had left out a great deal and she had to hear it.

He grimaced. 'Look, this is an old-fashioned part of the country. This isn't London, you know. People are years behind the rest of the country. I had to tell them who you were—they've seen Rory's studio, they've seen the pictures of you. They'd recognise you at once, just as I did, and when I said I'd invited you to stay they . . .'

'Were shocked?' she ended for him when he paused,
hesitating over the right word. 'Nice girls don't take their
clothes off for an artist, you mean? Well, I expected that
reaction. It's what I'd get if my own parents ever found
out. They don't know. I never told them what happened
in France that year. They were against the idea in the
first place—I had to nag them for months before they'd
let me take that job. They couldn't afford to send me to a
language school, you see, but I wanted to improve my
French and this seemed the best way, to learn while I
earned. We aren't a wealthy family, I needed the money,
but they thought it was too risky, a seventeen-year-old
going to France alone.' She made an angry face, her eyes
hard. 'And they were right! Not that I ever told them so
afterwards.' On the contrary, she had hidden the whole
story from them. They never knew what had hit her that
summer.

'Ormond must have been around thirty,' Oliver
thought aloud, his hands screwed into fists. 'What sort of
guy picks up a kid of seventeen and gets her to . . .' His
voice broke off as he saw Zoe turn scarlet. 'Anyway, he's
an unscrupulous, selfish . . .' That time he stopped
because he was so furious he couldn't come up with a
description violent enough, and she gave a choked, bitter
laugh. She had never been able to think of the right
description of Rory Ormond, either.

They were almost at the farmhouse and Oliver glanced
at it, then down at Zoe hurriedly. 'By the way, Lindy's at
the house. She just drove over and my mother asked her
to tea.'

'Was that her car, the little red sports car?'

He nodded. 'She drives it much too fast. I keep telling her she'll have an accident if she isn't careful, but she never listens to a word I say.'

Curiously, Zoe asked him, 'What did *she* say when you told her about me?'

'Funnily enough, she didn't say anything,' he said, frowning. 'She stared at me, then looked out of the window and went very quiet. I don't know if she was very surprised, or whether she's jealous of you.'

'Over you?' suggested Zoe, watching him out of the corner of her eyes.

He went red to his hairline. 'No, of course not! I meant over Ormond! I told you, I'm sure she hated seeing those pictures of you hanging in his studio. Whenever anyone said how good they were, Lindy would scowl and look sulky.' He caught Zoe's eye and defended: 'Well, she's only eighteen! You know how moody kids are at that age!'

'I suppose so,' said Zoe drily. She had begun to build up a picture of Lindy by now—the girl was obviously hopelessly spoilt and used to getting her own way. How many girls of that age had a jazzy little sports car to drive around in? Oliver said that Lindy's father doted on her, and she was an only child, used to the exclusive attention of her widowed father and not liking it if anyone else occupied the limelight Lindy liked to monopolise.

'If this is such an old-fashioned place, I'm surprised Lindy's father allows her to pose for Rory Ormond in the nude,' she remarked, and Oliver looked round at her, shock in his face.

'She doesn't! Not . . . in the nude, I mean. Or anyway . . .' He broke off, frowning, his face very red. 'Not that I know of. Did he tell you she had?' His eyes were alarmed.

'No, I just assumed from something you said . . .'

'You misunderstood me. No, George wouldn't hear of that.'

Her mouth tightened at the outrage in his voice. Oliver was horrifed by the very idea. He obviously shared his parents' views, and Zoe felt even less like walking into the farmhouse and facing people whose whole image of her came from the pictures she had been infatuated enough to pose for when she was just seventeen.

She had thought it was all over, buried in her past, a secret nobody would ever know. She had forgotten those paintings until she saw them again in that gallery in London, and even then it hadn't occurred to her that the people here in Scarlett would judge her on those canvases. She had been too impulsive in accepting Oliver's invitation; agreeing to his suggestion had seemed a good idea because it would kill two birds with one stone—rescue another girl from the sort of misery Rory had put her through and at the same time get some of her own back on Rory. It hadn't dawned on her until now that she wouldn't be a total stranger in this little village. These people would remember the paintings every time they looked at her. She winced at the realisation of what they would be thinking. Oliver had made it clear that she would be seen as a girl with a 'reputation'. No wonder they hadn't been too pleased to hear Oliver had brought her back here with him.

'Maybe I'd better not stay,' she said flatly.

'You must! I'm sure it's already starting to work,' Oliver told her, looking alarmed. 'Lindy wasn't pleased to hear I'd met you and I could see that Ormond had been taken by surprise. It's like throwing a stone into a pond—the ripples have begun! We mustn't give up now. Whatever happens, we must rescue Lindy.'

'Whatever happens?' Zoe asked with irony, but his face held no shadow of humour or understanding of her tone as he nodded vehemently.

'She's too young to realise the dangers of getting involved with someone like him. My God, he's old enough to be her father!

'Barely!' she protested. 'Thirty-seven isn't that old.'

'It is when you're eighteen. Her own father's only forty-two!'

'Then he ought to put his foot down. It's his job to rescue his daughter, not yours.'

'I told you, he won't because he thinks Rory Ormond's the best thing since the invention of oil-paints. George simply doesn't realise the harm Ormond could do her. He's stupid enough to trust Ormond.'

'Yes,' agreed Zoe, 'that is stupid.'

The dogs had sat down by the front door, their puzzled eyes on the two humans standing on the gravel path talking in low voices. Oliver looked at them and grinned, opened the door and let them run into the house.

'Come on, my parents will think we've got lost!' he said, and Zoe followed him into the hall. It was flagged with highly polished red stone on which Axminster mats had been strewn. Bowls of glowing ruby-red peonies and white carnations gave the air a summer perfume with a hint of musk. Oliver led her on to a door at the far end; it stood open, and a smell of hot bread floated out with a murmur of voices which broke off abruptly as the speakers realised Oliver and Zoe had arrived.

'Here we are,' said Oliver, nervously smiling. 'Mum, Dad, this is Zoe.'

The man seated at the well-scrubbed deal table stood up, took the pipe out of his mouth and laid it in an ashtray before coming forward to offer Zoe his gnarled hand. She smiled shyly, wishing she wasn't so flushed and obviously ill at ease.

John Naughton was grey-haired but solid, like an oak tree, with brawny arms and a barrel chest and a calm, patient, thoughtful face. Looking at him, Zoe could see exactly how Oliver would look in thirty years' time. She liked Mr Naughton at once, even though he gazed at her searchingly while they shook hands, without hiding that he was assessing the sort of person Zoe was and slowly looking more relieved as he realised she wasn't quite what he had been expecting. If Zoe hadn't been warned that Oliver's parents saw her in a lurid light she would have known at once from the way they stared at her.

Mrs Naughton was much smaller than either her husband or her son. She was plump and flushed, as fair-skinned as Oliver and surprisingly smooth-skinned, too, only a few lines around eye and mouth to betray that she was middle-aged. Her hair had been fair and was silvery now, her eyes were brown and gentle. A smile came into them belatedly as she and Zoe shook hands; by then Mrs Naughton had had time to decide that Zoe was really quite acceptable as a visitor.

'You must be tired after that long journey. I hate sitting in a car for hour after hour,' Mrs Naughton said, pulling out a chair from the table. 'Sit down, my dear. Do you mind eating in the kitchen? We always do, it's cosy in here.'

Zoe sat down. 'It's a charming room.' Her eyes wandered around the whitewashed walls, the red and white gingham curtains and the windowbox of geraniums on the windowsill outside, the tortoiseshell cat asleep on the seat of a chair, the rows of polished copper pans hanging next to a pine dresser full of pretty china plates and cups.

Her gaze stopped on a girl curled up in a chair on the other side of the room. Zoe knew it must be Lindy and stared. The other girl stared back openly, rudely. She had round, china-blue eyes and long brown hair. She was pretty, Zoe couldn't deny that. She was strikingly dressed in a tight-fitting pair of orange jeans and a white T-shirt under which she apparently wasn't wearing a thing, because her nipples showed through the taut material. Her lower lip pouted and she looked sullen.

'Zoe, this is Lindy,' said Oliver, looking worried.

'Hallo,' Zoe said to her, deliberately giving her a wide smile. It wasn't very sincere. It isn't easy to beam at someone who is glaring at you as if she would like to throw things at you, but Zoe had been brought up to be polite.

Lindy didn't answer, but she tossed her head. It could have been a nod of recognition. On the other hand it could just have been a toss of the head. Lindy left it to Zoe to decide.

'Nice to meet you, too,' said Zoe with another beam. She felt like asking the Naughtons, 'How long has she had a speech problem?' but decided they wouldn't think it very funny. All three of them were watching Lindy anxiously. Zoe got the feeling she had been spoilt from the minute she opened those saucer-like eyes on the world, and that she expected life to go on spoiling her for ever. Maybe it would. Or maybe Lindy was in for a sad surprise one of these days?

Zoe felt like going back to London and leaving Lindy to Rory Ormond's tender mercies. *He* would soon teach her that life was not a bowl of cherries!

'Well, shall we have tea, then?' Mrs Naughton asked brightly, producing a red and white gingham tablecloth which she flung over the deal table.

'Can I help?' asked Zoe, following her to the dresser from which she had begun to take plates.

'Oh, thank you, dear. I'll just make the tea, then. I've got the kettle on, it won't take a minute.'

When the table was laid with home-baked bread and scones, jam and whipped cream, a fruit cake and some thin cucumber sandwiches, they all sat down in an uneasy truce to begin eating. Oliver's parents asked Zoe occasional questions, trying to hide the fact that they were probing into her life, trying to sound very casual.

'You work in advertising, Oliver said. What sort of work is that, dear?' Mrs Naughton asked, and Zoe glanced round at a women's magazine which was flung down on a chair nearby. She leaned over, picked it up and opened it at a page of advertisements for cosmetics.

'This sort of copy is what I write,' she gestured, and they all stared at the page. 'And sometimes I write captions for pictures or the script for a TV ad.'

'How interesting,' said Mrs Naughton, pouring her some more tea. 'Have a scone, dear. I just made them.'

'Thank you. I love home-made scones. My mother makes them too.'

As fast as a beagle on the scent of a fox, Mrs Naughton asked, 'Where do your family live?'

'London,' Zoe told her, after she had swallowed the mouthful of scone. Mrs Naughton was watching her expectantly, waiting for more information, so she added calmly, 'My father's a teacher at a local school and my mother works there too, part-time, teaching needlework. My father teaches languages.'

'How interesting! And have you got any brothers and sisters?'

'One brother, Mike. He's six years older than me. He's married with two children.' Zoe felt like adding their names but realised that Mrs Naughton would be offended if she showed her irritation about being questioned so closely, so she just added, 'He lives in Sussex and has a smallholding.'

Mr Naughton pricked up his ears. 'Oh? Growing what?'

'Vegetables and flowers. He has quite a bit of land and three large greenhouses.'

'Hard work, that,' Mr Naughton remarked knowledgeably. 'Long hours, and you need a lot of help, picking and weeding. I prefer sheep, myself. They're always getting some disease and they die on you without warning, but they aren't as much work as vegetables. I worked on a smallholding when I was a lad. Up at dawn and hard at it until it got dark! Back-breaking work, that was, and little to show for it. Now with sheep you can make a fair living, stupid creatures though they are.'

'Not as silly as hens,' Mrs Naughton said, passing him

a large slice of fruit cake.

'No, hens are half-witted,' he agreed, and they forgot Zoe while they talked about hens they had known, some of their stories hilarious.

Lindy hadn't said a word so far, nor had she eaten anything. She had a cup of tea, which she sipped occasionally, but whenever she was offered food she shook her head with a grimace, as though eating was too mundane a process for her.

Zoe glanced at her as the Naughtons were talking and met hostile blue eyes. Lindy was making no secret of the fact that she did not like Zoe. Leaning forward suddenly, Lindy said, 'We all thought you were a professional model!'

Everyone around the table froze; you could have heard a pin drop. Lindy kept her eyes on Zoe's stiff face; the other girl was smiling maliciously, enjoying the sensation she had caused.

'We've all seen the paintings Rory did of you! I've often wondered—how did it feel, taking off your clothes to be painted? Weren't you embarrassed at all?'

Zoe's cold lips parted somehow. She could have hit the other girl. Lindy wanted to make a scene, embarrass her, but Zoe wasn't obliging her.

'Well,' she drawled, 'I was just a teenager at the time.' She paused, considering Lindy with pretended thought. 'Even younger than you, in fact,' she added softly.

Mr Naughton chuckled and Lindy threw him a furious glare, her small face dark red, and hit back at Zoe wildly.

'Did you have an affair with Rory?'

She had gone too far. The Naughtons were horrified and before Zoe could react, Mrs Naughton was on her

feet saying warmly to her: 'Zoe dear, I'll show you up to
your room and you can unpack your things.' She almost
propelled Zoe out of the room, and on the stairs she
looked back and said apologetically, 'Lindy's very
naughty, but as you said yourself, she's very young, and
she's got a bit of a crush on Rory Ormond at the moment.
Don't take any notice of her. I'll have a word with her
about her manners when I go back downstairs.'

Zoe had no need to answer because by then they had
reached the upper floor and Mrs Naughton was opening
a door into a charming bedroom decorated with Laura
Ashley prints on the walls and at the windows; the
delicate pink and blue colours were echoed in the carpet
and the woodwork was white. Zoe put down her suitcase
with a murmur of appreciation.

'What a lovely room!'

'I decorated it myself,' Mrs Naughton told her with
pleasure. 'I'm glad you like it.' She threw a last look
round the room. 'If there's anything you need, don't
hesitate to ask. The bathroom's through there. You'll be
sharing it with Oliver, but there's a bolt on each door.'
She backed to the door. 'I'll leave you to settle in, then.'

Left alone, Zoe unpacked and put her clothes away
and then went to wash and change into a rather more
chic outfit; a smooth-fitting coral silk dress with a plaited
belt which emphasised her tiny waist. The style was still
demure; a high, rolled collar and long billowing sleeves,
yet the way it clung was usually eye-riveting, as she knew
from experience. In her business, it was essential to look
good. She took a professional interest in her appearance
which wasn't so much vanity as cool self-appraisal, and a
permanent awareness of her effect in various clothes.

When she got downstairs, however, there was nobody around to admire her. The house seemed to be empty; there was no one in the kitchen and she couldn't hear a sound. She looked out of the front door and saw that the red sports car was no longer in the drive. Lindy had obviously gone off home in a temper, but where were the Naughtons? Going back into the kitchen, Zoe looked out of the window and thought she saw someone walking across the farmyard which was just visible through a fine screen of lilac trees, but whoever it was vanished behind an outbuilding. She hesitated, wondering if she should have put on jeans instead of a pretty dress. She would have gone to find her hosts, but the farmyard was littered with straw and mud and she was wearing delicate white high heels.

At that minute, she heard a door click and turned back into the hall, a smile ready, expecting to see Oliver or one of his parents.

When she saw who it was, her heart plummeted. Rory paused, mid-step, and stared back at her, his mouth mocking.

'What are you doing here?' Zoe attacked.

'Funny, I was about to ask you the same question!' He came on towards her and she had to fight down a strong desire to back away. He had changed into a lightweight summer suit; a cream linen weave with a very faint blue stripe in it. He looked good in it, and Zoe resented that, especially as she saw the way his grey eyes were wandering over her.

'What are you talking about?' she asked harshly, her mouth dry.

'I know how you met Oliver, but I'm still curious.

Don't try to kid me that when you two met it was love at first sight. I just don't buy it. Oliver isn't your type.'

'How would you know?' she retorted, bristling.

His mouth was crooked. 'I didn't know you for very long, but I knew you pretty well.'

She felt her throat close in shock and rage. If he had any decency he wouldn't mention what happened between them seven years ago, but then what had ever made her imagine Rory Ormond had any decency?

'So if it isn't love that's brought you all the way up here,' he drawled, 'what is it? What are you up to?'

CHAPTER THREE

ZOE took a sharp, unnerved breath. 'What do you mean?' Surely he hadn't guessed what lay behind Oliver's invitation to her? Did he know that Oliver was in love with Lindy, was that it? Oliver wasn't very good at hiding his feelings. *She* had guessed his secret almost from the first moment he mentioned Lindy, and she had only just met him. Rory had known him for some time and had had plenty of opportunity for observing him; he wouldn't have missed the sort of clues Oliver left around with every word, every look he gave Lindy. Rory was a trained observer of people; she had often been struck by his ability to read faces.

He was watching her, now, his grey eyes acute. 'It seems an odd coincidence that you should get so friendly with Oliver after running into him at my exhibition,' he observed.

She got herself under control, her facial muscles tight. 'He noticed that I was upset when I saw those pictures and he followed me out of the gallery. I suppose it was a coincidence that he happened to be there at the same time, but then life is full of little coincidences.'

'Isn't it?' Rory said drily.

'And talking about the exhibition,' Zoe went on, deciding that attack was the best defence, 'I want you to remove those pictures of me from it. How do you think I feel, knowing that anyone can just walk in there and see me naked?'

'The exhibition closes in two days,' he told her brusquely. 'Don't change the subject.'

'I'm not. That is the subject—you had a nerve, putting those paintings on display!'

'Don't be so narrow-minded. They're beautiful, why be ashamed of your body? It's a work of art in its own right, and the paintings I did of it are probably the work I'm proudest of.' Rory was looking annoyed now; his eyes glacial and his jaw rigid. 'Some of the greatest works of art in the world are representations of the human body. Do you feel embarrassed when you see a Greek statue or Michelangelo's David? Do you want them hidden from sight, too?'

Flushed and agitated, Zoe said, 'That's different!'

'Why?' he challenged, and she stared at him helplessly, her tongue paralysed and her brain coming up with nothing.

Rory laughed shortly. 'You see? You're making a silly fuss about nothing!'

'I am not!' she snapped, suddenly able to speak again, and trembling with rage. 'When I posed for you I was too young to realise what I was letting myself in for! If you asked me today, I'd refuse to pose like that. I don't want strangers staring at me in the nude—I hate the idea. Other women may not mind, but I do. I'm a very different person from the girl you knew. I'm a successful career-woman now . . .'

'Career-woman?' he interrupted, brows swooping upwards. 'You?'

Her teeth met. When she could unglue them she said

forcibly, 'Yes, a career-woman! I'm in advertising.'

'You call that a career? What do you sell, soap?'

'I'm a copy-writer. I work on a number of campaigns!' Her dignified tone didn't seem to cut much ice with him; he was still grinning, but Zoe ignored his amusement. She went on crisply, 'If it got out that I'd posed for that sort of picture, people would talk. It would give people the wrong idea of me.'

'By people you mean men?'

She lifted her chin. 'Some men would think it was okay to make a heavy pass at me after seeing your paintings, yes!'

His mouth twisted. 'And you couldn't cope with that?'

She was getting angrier. 'Why should I have to? When I arrived here the Naughtons were very dubious about me and very worried because Oliver had brought me home with him. They didn't say much, but they stared, and I knew why! Oliver says they're old-fashioned and maybe they are, but I can't blame them for what they thought. They don't want their only son dating a girl who takes her clothes off to pose for artists.'

'Did they throw you out of the house?' he asked coolly.

'Obviously they didn't, but . . .'

'Did they tell Oliver never to darken their door again?'

'Oh, don't be absurd!'

'I know the Naughtons pretty well,' Rory said drily. 'They may have been taken aback when Oliver produced you out of the blue, but I'm sure they were very kind and hospitable to you after they'd got over their first amazement.'

'Of course they were, but all the same, it was embarrassing for me at first.'

'You seem to have recovered from it well enough!' He surveyed her from head to toe with a crooked smile.' You were quite something when you were seventeen, you know.'

Zoe swallowed, looking away. The irritation seeped out of her and she felt her heart begin to thud in a slow, heavy way that disturbed her. Rory was turning his potent sexual charm on her, she recognised the signals immediately in the little twist of the mouth, the half-lidded grey eyes glimmering intimately, the husky, dropped voice. At seventeen she hadn't had a clue how he was making her head spin; she only knew he could to it with a look, a smile, a murmured word. Now she was an experienced adult and she was well aware of the ingredients in his devastating cocktail, but that didn't seem to stop its effects. All the telltale physical symptoms showed up; her mouth going dry, her pulses racing, her skin turning hot.

'But you're even lovelier now,' Rory added softly, and her ears buzzed with hypertension, until she heard him add thoughtfully, 'Yes, I must paint you again. It would be fascinating, putting the changes on canvas, I think I'd . . .'

'You aren't painting me again,' Zoe erupted hoarsely. 'Never again!'

'Is that a dare?' he asked, his eyes gleaming.

'No!' she denied hurriedly, her blood running cold at that excitement.

'I never back down from a challenge,' Rory murmured silkily, his smile a deliberate mockery. 'What do I get if I win the dare?'

'You aren't painting me,' she said helplessly, retreating

in the face of his teasing. He might think it was funny to bait her like that, but she felt it as a threat and she was deeply relieved to hear the back door opening, the sound of voices floating across the kitchen. The Naughtons were back. They scraped their boots noisily as they talked and laughed.

'I came to invite you and Oliver to a party,' Rory said coolly in a very different tone. The taut atmosphere between them had shattered and Zoe could breathe again. Before she could answer, Rory had moved past her into the kitchen and she heard him talking to the Naughtons in a friendly, casual way. Zoe didn't listen. She was thinking about him and feeling bewildered because the way she felt was so changeable and complex. She had come here hating him, prepared to do what she could to hit back at him. She had forgotten too many things about Rory Ormond that she was now beginning to remember—she had begun to realise that the moment she first saw him again, on the cliff. Alarm bells had rung inside her head then. They were ringing even louder now.

When she walked into the kitchen, Oliver grinned at her. 'How do you feel about going to a barbecue tomorrow?'

Under Rory's watchful eyes she could only shrug and smile back. 'Up to you, Oliver. If you want to go, I'm happy about it.'

'Isn't that nice?' Rory drawled sarcastically, and a few moments later he left.

Zoe helped Mrs Naughton get the supper and after the meal they sat around for a while, talking, before having an early night. Zoe was exhausted after the long drive from London and was glad to get to bed. She gathered that the Naughtons always went to bed early. They had to be up at first light to start feeding their various animals, Oliver told her.

Next day, Oliver drove her around to give her a glimpse of his part of Cumbria. They drove into Whitehaven and did some shopping for Mrs Naughton, drove inland and followed winding roads among the Cumbrian hills for an hour to catch a glimpse of Hadrian's Wall, but they had promised to be back for lunch by one, so Oliver promised to take her to the Wall another day, and headed home.

'Who's giving the barbecue tonight?' Zoe asked as they were walking back into the farmhouse.

'Maggie,' Oliver told her. 'She runs a riding stables, on the other side of the village.'

'Maggie's a dear,' Mrs Naughton said warmly later. 'You'll love her. If you're going to the barbecue tonight you won't be wanting dinner, so I'll save these chops for tomorrow.'

'I'd forgotten the barbecue,' said Zoe frowning. 'What should I wear? I haven't brought many clothes, just jeans and tops mostly.'

'They'll be fine,' Mr Naughton assured her, but Oliver shook his head.

'No, wear that pretty dress you wore last night. It suits you.'

His parents exchanged smiling glances, but Zoe caught the look in Oliver's eyes and knew it wasn't for his benefit that he wanted her to wear the coral-red dress. A flush crept into her face and the Naughtons chuckled, completely misunderstanding.

'And keep your eyes open,' Mrs Naughton told Oliver.

'I'm dying to know how much truth there is in the gossip.'

'What gossip?'

'Maggie and Rory!' Mrs Naughton told him, and Zoe jerked to attention. Oliver looked just as dumbfounded as she felt; he shot Zoe a sideways glance, his eyes dilated.

'Maggie and Rory? You're joking!'

'Why not?' Mrs Naughton bridled, her face indignant. 'Maggie Thorn's seven years younger than Rory and she's a very nice woman. I've always liked Maggie. She nursed that mother of hers without a syllable of complaint, although Joan Thorn was a very irritating woman and wouldn't let Maggie have any sort of life of her own all those years. We tried to help Maggie all we could, but Joan hated her to go out. It must have been a weary time, especially over the last year or two when Joan was really ill, but Maggie never showed any sign of strain until it was all over and she went to pieces.'

Oliver had looked increasingly impatient as his mother talked, and as soon as she drew breath he asked, 'But what on earth makes you think that there's anything between her and Ormond?'

His mother gave him a triumphant nod. 'You know Maggie—have you ever seen her except in riding clothes or jeans and a shirt? Never had her hair done or put on make-up; washed her face with oatmeal soap and pulled her hair back off her face and tied it in a ponytail. Always out in the fresh air, however bad the weather—her skin was like tanned leather. Well, I saw her in the village last week and I hardly recognised her. She was wearing a smart new dress, she'd had her hair done and she looked a million dollars. Everyone's been talking about the way she's changed. Don't tell me there isn't a man in her life,

either, because no woman has the sort of sparkle Maggie
had last week unless she's in love!'

'But what makes you think it's Ormond?' Oliver asked
dazedly.

'He's always at the stables, that's why! Everyone has
seen him there. His car's always parked in the drive. And
who else could it be? He's the only bachelor of the right
age in the village!'

Mr Naughton interrupted impatiently. 'Oliver, are you
going to give me a hand with those hoggets?' and the two
men disappeared out of the house. Zoe helped Mrs
Naughton hunt for eggs which her free-range hens had
laid in strange places. As they wandered around the
garden and the hens scattered, squawking. Mrs
Naughton talked about Oliver happily while Zoe thought
about Rory Ormond and wondered with a peculiar
uneasiness if the rumour about him and the unknown
Maggie had any truth beind it. If he was involved with
her, why should he risk a flirtation with Lindy? Zoe
winced at the thought of how badly hurt an older woman
might be if she discovered that the man she was in love
with was secretly involved with a girl more than ten years
younger than herself. The wound inflicted would be far
worse than that made by any other infidelity, it would
undermine the older woman's sense of identity, rip her
ego to shreds.

'How old did you say Maggie Thorn was?' she asked
Mrs Naughton, who cheerfully changed the direction of
her chatter to tell her.

'Thirty-one, I think—or is it thirty-two? She should
have been married ten years ago, but that mother of hers
had a heart attack every time there was talk of a

wedding, so the man married someone else and went to Yorkshire to raise pigs. Oh, Joan Thorn was a selfish woman. She wanted Maggie waiting on her hand and foot and running those stables into the bargain, to pay the bills. I'd never have put up with it, but Maggie's soft-hearted.'

Zoe was very sorry for Maggie Thorn if she was in love with Rory Ormond. From the sound of it, Maggie deserved something better than a man capable of callous selfishness—she had already suffered enough from a mother with the same insistent egotism. Or did she have some sort of masochistic urge to sacrifice herself to someone's ego? Zoe grimaced. There were women like that; women for whom happiness meant abandonment to someone else's will. During the summer when Zoe was in Provence she had been so crazy about Rory Ormond that she knew she would have done anything he asked of her, and it made her violently angry to remember that now.

Oliver was hard at work somewhere on the farm all that afternoon and Zoe kept busy helping his mother, fascinated by this glimpse of the life of a farmer's wife. You needed lots of energy, she decided ruefully later, as she lay back in a scented bath, her tired muscles slowly relaxing. Closing her eyes, she let her mind wander, but that was a mistake because it inevitably began to dwell on Rory Ormond. It seemed so incredible to imagine him marrying.

Her eyes flew open as she felt a queer little stab in the region of her diaphragm. Indigestion! she told herself hurriedly. She had eaten a heavy farm lunch and then spent a long time bending down to peer under bushes and trees in search of eggs.

Climbing out of the bath, she caught sight of herself in the mirror, immediately reminded of Rory's painting of her and wished she hadn't been going to this barbecue. But if she didn't go, Rory might think she was afraid to see him, and she couldn't let him think that. He had no power over her any more, and she meant him to know that.

When she came downstairs she found Oliver waiting for her. He was ready too; wearing a blue cotton sweater which suited his fair skin, with white denims and casual shoes. He looked his best in the open air; his broad-shouldered, healthy appearance had been out of place in London, but here he perfectly suited his background.

He looked admiringly at her, smiling. 'You look terrific!'

'Thank you,' she said, smiling back, and his parents watched them with open interest and approval. During that day, Mrs Naughton had totally come to terms with Zoe and forgotten all her reservations about her.

As they drove through a slowly dropping twilight Oliver turned and said excitedly, 'Can it be true about Maggie Thorn and Ormond? I hadn't heard a whisper and I'd swear Lindy hasn't, either. Do you think I should drop her a hint?'

Drily, Zoe said, 'I should wait until you know how much fire there is behind the smoke. If you tell Lindy too soon and it turns out to be pure nonsense, it may do more harm than good.'

'I wonder if Lindy's been invited to this barbecue,' pondered Oliver a moment later, but since Zoe didn't know the answer to the question she didn't say anything and they both lapsed into silence for a while.

They passed through the little village centre; a winding street of grey stone houses with here and there a few shops, several public houses, their signs swinging in a breeze which had sprung up, and a small church with a beautifully proportioned steeple. Zoe caught sight of the carved heads of saints above the ancient oak door and turned to peer backwards.

'How old is your church?' she asked.

'Thirteenth century,' Oliver said vaguely.

'I must visit it while I'm here; it looks interesting. I love the carvings.'

'There are some fascinating gargoyles on the guttering, too,' he agreed, still looking abstracted. She didn't need three guesses at what he was thinking about. Oliver was in love; even if he wouldn't admit it. He was always thinking about Lindy. Zoe couldn't understand it. The girl might be pretty, but it was a skin-deep beauty; her face was full of baby softness, she pouted and scowled with childish inability to control herself. What was it Rory Ormond saw in her?

What had he seen in Zoe? That summer seven years ago he had spent so many hours drawing and painting her, but when she saw those pictures again in London she had been taken aback to remember how very young she herself had been. Rory had shown that with merciless clarity; catching the undeveloped adult in the turn of the head, the curve of cheek and jaw, the young throat and mouth. He had drawn a child on the way to becoming a woman and had done it with obsessive fascination.

Was that what he was looking for in Lindy, too? Perhaps, she conceded grimly. Artists do have a tendency to be obsessed with one particular subject, one particular idea—coming back to it again and again throughout their lives. Who could say why one thing rather than another captured their imagination?

They saw the barbecue before they actually turned into the drive up to the riding stables. The sky was giving off a reddish glow behind the solid stone and brickwork of the buildings; sparks flew up from a bonfire and they could smell charcoal smoke from the barbecue itself.

'I'm getting hungry already,' said Oliver, parking behind another car with care. There were quite a few people here, judging by the number of cars parked in the drive, and as they walked through the stableyard they heard voices and laughter from a paddock not far away. From the loose boxes behind closed doors they heard shuffling and heavy breathing; the horses were aware that something unusual was going on around the stables and they were restless.

Dusk had descended by then; the figures around the bonfire took on strange shapes as the flames leapt up and died down. Someone was setting up a loudspeaker system so that they could have music; Zoe recognised the outline of Rory's body on a stepladder, fixing the loudspeaker to a tree, while a woman in red velvet trousers and a loose white lace top stood below, holding the ladder and giving him instructions.

'There's Maggie,' Oliver said, and the woman turned her head to look at him. She had a thin, pleasant face and warm, reddish brown hair which was cut short, curling thickly over her head. Her eyes seemed dark in the firelight, but as she turned to greet them Zoe saw that they were actually sherry-brown.

'Maggie, this is Zoe Stroud. She's staying with us. I hope it's all right to bring her.'

'Rory said he'd invited you both,' Maggie Thorn said cheerfully, then held out a hand to Zoe. 'Hallo, welcome to Scarlett. I hope you're enjoying your visit. This is such a lovely part of England, and we're all very proud of it. You must get Oliver to take you to Hadrian's Wall and down the Lakes. We've got a positive armoury of beauty spots! Or have you been here before? Am I preaching to the converted?'

'No, this is my first visit, but I'd love to get to know Cumbria better.'

'Then you're in for a wonderful time,' said Maggie, her smile revealing two dimples in her tanned cheeks.

'Maggie gets a lot of tourists at the stables,' Rory said, climbing down and surveying his handiwork with satisfaction. 'She's very good at selling our countryside to newcomers.' He grinned teasingly at Maggie. 'There, that should work fine now. Try it.'

Maggie vanished, and a moment later music streamed out over their heads and people turned to listen, exclaiming with surpise. It was far too loud; Maggie turned the volume down until it was merely a pleasant background noise to the party chatter.

'Can I get you a drink?' Rory asked.

'I'll get it, what would you like, Zoe?' Oliver gave her a quick, secretive look, a silent message she grasped impatiently and was unable to argue with in front of Rory.

'I don't mind,' she said and Oliver nodded, hurrying away. Zoe stared after him, thinking he was being rather obvious, leaving her alone with Rory like that, until she noticed some new arrivals coming through the open gate into the paddock. Lindy! She might have known!

She gave Rory a glance, but he hadn't apparently noticed that Lindy had arrived. He was watching Zoe, his mouth crooked.

'Firelight suits you.'

She gave him a sarcastic smile. 'Does it?' She didn't pretend to believe him. 'I don't have a fireplace in London; the smokeless zone means we have to have artificial heating. My flat is fitted with off-peak electric central heating, very expensive to run, even so. I don't have it on if I can help it.'

'Where do you live?'

'St John's Wood.'

'A block of flats?'

She shook her head. 'We have a ground-floor flat in a large house.'

Rory's brows met; black and formidable above his arrogant nose. 'We?' he queried.

'I share the flat,' Zoe expanded without telling him any more than that.

'Male or female flatmate?' He insisted on knowing and she was tempted to tell him it was a man, but found it hard to lie.

'Female,' she admitted reluctantly, and his eyes gleamed with amusement.

'Is Oliver the only man in your life?'

'Why should I tell you that?' she retorted.

'Why shouldn't you?'

'None of your business,' she said crossly, even more reluctant to admit that there had never been a man in her life who meant anything much to her. Never since she was seventeen, anyway. Rory Ormond had cured her of romantic dreams, but she hadn't been able to settle for anything less and so she had drifted from one unsatisfactory relationship to another without giving anything of herself to any of the men she briefly dated. It wasn't simply that she didn't care for casual sex or didn't find any man attractive enough—she was terrified of getting hurt again and backed off long before she reached the point of caring about anyone.

Rory had watched her intently, his eyes narrowed as he tried to probe behind her taut face. He was clever and dangerous; he saw too much, and Zoe wanted to keep him at a distance. She looked anxiously around for Oliver and saw him over by the bonfire with Lindy and another man in a cord jacket and matching trousers. In the flare of the flames Zoe got a sudden glimpse of a head of rough black curls, a sturdy body, a bony profile. Could that be Lindy's father? He didn't look old enough, but then Oliver had said George was in his early forties, hadn't he? This man could be that age.

'When did you start working in advertising?' Rory asked, and she looked back at him reluctantly.

'After I left college.'

'So you did get to university?' He sounded wry, she couldn't think why. 'And got a degree?'

She nodded, looking away again because it bothered her to be alone with him all this time, especially when he kept asking her questions. So far he hadn't touched on really treacherous ground, but Zoe was afraid that any minute he would. She didn't trust him; he might decide to amuse himself by teasing her again, and she couldn't be sure enough of her self-command to risk that.

Whether she lost her temper or her head, it would be equally risky.

'Oliver's taking a long time to get me that drink!' she said uneasily.

'Oliver's otherwise occupied,' drawled Rory, his eyes flicking towards the bonfire and then she realised that he had known all along that Lindy was here.

'She's pretty, isn't she?' Zoe asked, watching him.

'Very.' Their eyes met and she felt confused, her neck beating with a fierce pulse.

'I gather you're painting her?' she managed to say huskily.

'I've almost finished the portrait her father commissioned.'

Zoe's eyes widened. 'He commissioned it?'

'I only paint the occasional portrait, it isn't my favourite medium, but George is a friend and when he asked me to paint his daughter for him I couldn't very well refuse.' Rory's grey eyes mocked her. 'George will be thrilled to meet you. He admires the portraits I did of you; that was what gave him the idea of getting me to paint his daughter.' He paused, looking across the paddock at the bonfire and the silhouettes of Oliver, Lindy and the man in grey cords. 'By the way, don't tell anyone this—the portrait is a present for Lindy's birthday next autumn. She doesn't know I've painted it for her father, she's busy trying to persuade him to buy it and me to sell it!'

'Oliver doesn't know about it?' Zoe said slowly, less a question than a statement of fact. She knew perfectly well that Oliver didn't know the reason why Rory was painting the other girl. If he had known, she wouldn't be

here! Or would she? Did it make any difference *why*
Rory was painting the girl? As far as Oliver was
concerned, Lindy was seeing Rory far too often, she was
head over heels in love with him, whether he or her father
knew it. But Rory must know it; he was far too intelligent
to have missed the fact, and he must have given her
plenty of encouragement or he would have put an end to
their lengthy sessions. Rory could be ruthless when he
was tired of someone.

Her stomach clenched and she took a deep, harsh
breath. Rejection was hard to forget; it cut too deep into
the ego and left too many scars.

'They're starting to dance,' Rory murmured close to
her. 'Shall we? Or would you rather join the crowd
around the barbecue? The steaks and beefburgers should
be ready now—I can smell them from here.'

So could Zoe and she wished she hadn't lost her
appetite because faced with a choice between dancing
with Rory and forcing herself to eat food she didn't really
want, she had no real option but to go for the latter.
Nothing would persuade her to join the couples dancing
close to the bonfire. She wasn't letting Rory put his arms
round her.

'I'm starving,' she lied. 'I think I'll join the queue for a
steak.'

'Okay, I'll ask Lindy to dance,' Rory accepted
amiably, turning to move towards the bonfire, and Zoe
stared after him. Was that what he had wanted all along?
Had he been waiting for a chance to join Lindy?

She began to walk across the tussocky grass, moving
much too fast on such uneven ground. Her ankle twisted
suddenly, on what felt like a small molehill. She could

have saved herself with a lurch to one side, but she let herself tumble forward with a loud exclamation.

Rory reached her a moment later. 'Have you hurt yourself?' he asked, sounding genuinely concerned as he helped her back on her feet.

Zoe was hating herself. Why had she done that? She didn't care if he danced with Lindy or not, and if Oliver had any brains he would have been dancing with Lindy already, making sure that Rory couldn't snatch her from him.

She had to go on pretending, leaning on the arm he had slid around her, all her weight on one foot as she lifted the other and stared down at it.

'It's nothing,' she said. 'Just a little sprain. I didn't see a molehill in the dark.'

Rory let go of her and knelt to inspect her ankle. In one way she was relieved because it had been nerve-racking to have his arm round her, but it was hardly less disturbing to feel his cool fingers gently pressing her foot, exploring the extent of the damage. Taking a deep breath, she watched the black head bent over her ankle.

'I see you still have very small feet,' he murmured as he slid her shoe back on, but he didn't get up right away, his eyes travelled slowly up her long, slim legs, and Zoe had a problem breathing as that gaze skated over her hips and waist, past the rapid rise and fall of her high breasts. Rory's face was half-masked by shadow, but Zoe instinctively knew that he was seeing her body without the silky tights and the clinging coral pink dress. Heat swept up her face and she wanted to hit him, her hands curling into fists at her side.

'Don't look at me like that!' she burst out before she could stop herself.

'Like what?' he asked softly, getting to his feet.

Hot-cheeked, she knew she couldn't put it into words and so did he, the wicked glimmer of his eyes taunting her with her frustrated impotence.

Oliver joined them a moment later, his face anxious. 'I saw you fall over, Zoe—are you okay? This part of the paddock is very uneven ground, much wiser to stay near the fire.'

'I'm fine,' she said huskily.

'Just a little out of breath,' Rory added, still tormenting her, but she ignored him. It was wonderful to have a sense of humour, no doubt, but she wished he wouldn't exercise it at her expense.

Oliver had brought Lindy and the man in grey cords over to them. 'Zoe, you remember Lindy, don't you?' Oliver said uncertainly, his expression making it clear that it was Lindy's attitude to her that worried him rather than her attitude to Lindy.

Zoe gave Lindy a polite smile. 'Of course. Hallo again.'

Lindy glowered, but Zoe pretended not to notice.

'And this is Lindy's father, George Ash. George, Zoe Stroud.'

Zoe liked George Ash the minute their eyes met; his were blue and deep-set, fringed with sooty black lashes, their expression warm and friendly.

'I don't need an introduction, I'd know you anywhere,' he said, taking both her hands and holding them while he gazed at her. 'It's fascinating,' he said slowly. 'Fascinating. You're different, yet the little changes haven't altered the basic face Rory painted. He caught the whole human being, not just the surface.' His eyes flicked sideways to Rory, his grin rueful and full of respect and admiration. 'You clever swine!'

'Thanks,' said Rory with amusement. 'I was just telling her that I'd like to paint her again to capture the changes and the bedrock personality that hasn't altered an inch.'

George Ash's face lit up and he squeezed Zoe's hands before dropping them. 'Now that's a marvellous idea! You must do it, Rory. First the girl, then the woman.'

Zoe's teeth were gritted together; she didn't say anything, but her rebellious eyes flashed at Rory, whose mockery deepened.

Lindy was looking furious, too. 'He can't paint anything else until he's finished my portrait. You won't have time, will you, Rory?'

'I've more or less finished with you,' Rory said casually, and Zoe's heart contracted as she watched the younger girl's face. Did she realise yet that Rory meant that in more ways than one? His art and his life were inextricably entwined, as far as the opposite sex went. While he was painting Zoe she had been convinced he was as much in love with her as she had been with him, but when he had used her up in his work he was finished with her personally too.

Poor Lindy, she thought, half angry, half compassionate—how will she take it once she realises it's all over? She was older than Zoe had been when it happened to her; yet somehow Zoe had a strong suspicion that Lindy wouldn't cope too well with the pain of rejection. She was too cherished and indulged; she had never been denied anything, and her angry, demanding stare at Rory held bewilderment too. Lindy didn't believe he could mean it!

'When am I going to see it?' asked George Ash, lit up and excited, and blithely unaware of his daughter's feelings.

'When I'm quite satisfied,' Rory said, grinning at him. 'Be patient, George, not long now.' He turned to Lindy, his tone softening. 'Come and dance,' he commanded, and she glowed as she put her hand into his and went off with him across the grass.

Zoe stared after them bitterly. So Rory hadn't quite decided to drop Lindy?

'He's a genius, you know,' George Ash said dreamily, his own eyes on the pair who had now begun to dance in the glow of the firelight. The turf around the bonfire had been carefully rolled flat to make it safe to dance, but most people had drifted away to get food from the barbecue site; Lindy and Rory Ormond were almost the only dancers left for the moment.

'I wish to God I had half his talent,' George added, running spatulate fingers through his mop of curls. His enthusiasm and eagerness made him seem far younger than forty-two, but Zoe suddenly noticed a couple of streaks of grey among the rough black hair. 'I know just enough about art to realise I'm hopeless,' he said, grinning at her. 'I've got the technique to imitate but no creativity worth mentioning, unfortunately. I'd give my eye teeth to be Rory Ormond. He's still young, he's got a lifetime of work ahead of him, but he's so damned good already.' He groaned, tugging at his curls with both hands to express his feelings. 'If I didn't like him so much, I'd hate him!'

'Don't sell yourself short!' Maggie Thorn said suddenly behind him, and they all looked at her in surprise, not having noticed her joining them. Her eyes sparkled with impatience in the firelight as she looked at George. 'You're a wonderful teacher, you inspire those kids at the school to do quite amazing work. Look at that exhibition last year! You said yourself that the standard was surprisingly high for that age-group! They couldn't have done it without you; you make people stretch further than they ever would have done by themselves.'

George was blushing like a schoolboy. 'Oh, shucks,' he muttered, shuffling his feet. 'Now I'll have to ask you to dance, lord help you! I hope you're wearing sturdy shoes, Maggie. You know I can't help dancing on other people's feet!'

'You make me so mad I could slap you sometimes,' she said crossly, letting him lead her away by the hand.

'The queue at the barbecue is much shorter,' Oliver gloomily informed Zoe. 'Let's get some food while there's still some left.' He hadn't suggested that they dance, for which she was thankful, but she still didn't feel hungry. The thought of food nauseated her. She felt hollow inside and light-headed too, and she hated Rory Ormond more than ever. He was an unprincipled, ruthless, cold-hearted egomaniac, and if that made him a genius in George Ash's scheme of things, Zoe couldn't help thinking that George must have made a mistake somewhere.

When she and Oliver had collected their food they stood around the barbecue, their plates in their hands, talking to other people. Oliver kept introducing her to someone and Zoe found it hard to remember any names, but they were all friendly and it wasn't a problem chatting lightly to them. It helped to keep her mind off

Rory Ormond, anyway. Oliver asked her to dance some time later. By that time, most of the guests were either dancing or talking by the bonfire since all the food had been eaten. Zoe kept a wary eye on Rory and Lindy, who were laughing in a large group around George Ash and Maggie, and Oliver followed her gaze, frowning.

'You see what I mean? Lindy can't keep her eyes off him.'

'I noticed,' accepted Zoe. 'She doesn't like Maggie much, does she?'

'Jealous of her,' Oliver grimaced.

'Do you *really* think there's something going on between Maggie Thorn and Rory?' Zoe hadn't yet seen any signs of it. They were at ease with each other, they smiled and talked casually, but Zoe had seen no intimate glances, none of the telltale little signs which betray a private relationship.

'I've never noticed it,' Oliver disdained. 'It's all my mother's idea! In a small place like this there's always a lot of gossip.'

Zoe nodded, but she remained uncertain and curious, and when they stopped dancing to join the others by the fire she kept watching Rory talking to Maggie and Lindy, his expression unreadable. If he was more interested in one than the other, she couldn't tell.

Looking at her watch, she realised it was getting late, almost midnight, the music had been turned down low and the bonfire was sinking. The party would be over soon, but people seemed in no hurry to leave, they stood about talking in groups while some helped Maggie to clear away the barbecue. Oliver and Zoe carried a number of glasses into the house for her and Oliver helped to stack the dishwasher while Zoe went back for the rest of the glasses.

It was still very hot, even humid, and people looked at the sky saying, 'A storm on the way, don't you think?' But they still showed no eagerness to break up the party, even when a low rumble of thunder sounded over some woods on the skyline and a flash of lightning warned that the storm was actually heading towards them. Zoe watched the sky split with a sudden flash and decided that it wouldn't break overhead for another hour or so, but she was wrong.

The rain began suddenly ten minutes later; a torrential downpour with the force of a jungle storm, turning the dry paddock ground into mud within minutes, and sending everyone running for cover. It was impossible to see clearly in the violence of the storm, and Zoe had lost Oliver. People climbed into cars, slammed doors, began to back out of the riding-stable driveway; others sheltered under the eaves of the stables or stood in the kitchen doorway of the house, but she couldn't see Oliver among them. Had he gone to his car, she wondered, running in that direction, her dress saturated almost at once and clinging wetly to her body. She hadn't brought a coat, her hair felt like damp string and water dripped down her neck, making her shiver.

It was dark in the drive except when headlights blinded her. A horn blared right behind her and she instinctively leapt out of the way to let a car drive past. It plunged through a muddy puddle and sprayed her from the waist downwards with dirty water. Almost in tears, Zoe stood back in the side of the drive, peering through the dark and the rain for any sign of Oliver or his car.

It was a second later that a car drew up beside her and the passenger door swung open. She climbed in thankfully, out of breath and convulsively shivering.

'I thought you'd gone without me!' She turned a dripping face to the driver and stiffened in shock. It wasn't Oliver; it was Rory, and before she could get out another word he drove off with a squeal of tyres.

CHAPTER FOUR

'OLIVER must be looking for me,' she said hurriedly. 'His car is somewhere down here—could you stop when you see it?'

Rory didn't answer, nor did he stop along the drive. He kept going and turned into the lane behind another car from the party. Looking at him sideways, Zoe bit her lip.

'It's nice of you to give me a lift, but Oliver will be worried.'

'I told him I'd take care of you,' Rory said. 'He's taking Lindy and her father—their car wouldn't start. Some rain got into the engine, I expect.'

'Oh, I see,' mumbled Zoe, wondering why he hadn't taken Lindy and George Ash instead of leaving it to Oliver, or had Oliver preferred it that way? She turned her head to peer out of the rain-washed window. There was little to see of the countryside through the driving storm; a grey stone wall here, a cottage there, otherwise there was just darkness and rain, except when the lightning crashed down from the sky. She didn't remember this road from the trip to the party, but then this landscape was all rolling hills and green pasture. There weren't many landmarks to recognise.

'Did you enjoy the party?' he asked, and she turned to look at him, startled.

'Yes, very much. They're friendly people, aren't they?'

'This is a small community. People get to know each

other better than Londoners usually do.' Rory turned left
and changed gear, his hand briefly brushing her thigh,
and Zoe felt a deep shudder run over her whole body
while at the same time her face burned as if she had a
fever. She couldn't pretend, even to herself, that she
didn't understand what was making her feel as if she
were in the throes of some terrible illness, but the
admission made her angry with herself. Was she out of
her mind to feel like this about a man she despised and
distrusted? Her physical sensations were, if anything,
more intense than they had been when she was
seventeen, yet neither her mind nor her heart was
involved this time, and she fought rigidly to get her own
sensuality under control.

'What did you think of Maggie?' he asked lightly, and
she swallowed, trying to think straight.

'She ... she's very pleasant.' She must stop being
aware of him; she had to think of something else. Yet in
the intimacy of the dark car with the rain pelting down
on the roof and against the windscreen that was easier
said than done. This was what she had been afraid of
from the minute she saw him again. It had been one thing
to plan how she would confront him, before she came
down here—in London she hadn't realised how strong
the tug of his attraction would be.

Her eyes darkened with bewilderment. How could you
want so badly someone you did not even like? Her inbuilt
beliefs meant that she expected love to be mixed up with
desire, but she would never feel real emotion for Rory
Ormond again and she was humiliated by the violent
responses of her senses. How could she feel like this? She
simply couldn't understand it.

Was it because seven years ago he had ended their affair abruptly, without warning, and her feelings towards him had not had time to die naturally as they would have done if they had been the same age and it had been a boy-and-girl love? That was what most people went through on their journey to maturity—a brief, tempestuous adolescent passion; a foreshadowing of the real thing to follow, something too hot to last.

Instead, Rory had vanished, and the only way she could deal with her pain and love was to seal it and put it into deep-freeze where it couldn't hurt her any longer. She had turned all her attention to her studies and then to work, and she hadn't let any other man get near her. Love had terrified her; it still did, she admitted, closing her eyes with a shiver.

She had learnt to hate Rory, but she hadn't ever really coped with what was left of that bitter, intense desire, had she?

Was that why she felt like this? Was that hunger, hidden away inside her, still alive?

The car had turned into a sunken lane between deep, high stone walls which made it look like a dark tunnel down which the wind roared and the rain beat furiously. Staring out blankly, Zoe suddenly wondered where they were. She didn't recognise this road.

'Where are we?' she asked nervously, turning her head to look at Rory.

Without answering, he turned into a drive, slowed to a halt for a moment and then drove on as the garage door in front of which he had pulled up rose silently to allow them to enter. Sitting up in shock, Zoe realised he had operated some electronic device which opened and shut

the door. She also realised that this was not Oliver's
farmhouse. But before she could say or do anything she
saw the garage door descending as silently and Rory
switched off the engine, got out of the car and came
round to open her door.

She stayed in her seat, staring furiously at him. 'Is this
your house? Will you take me back to Oliver's home,
please? He'll be wondering where I am.'

'He won't be there yet. He has to drive Lindy and her
father home and then get back to the farm, and that will
take him an hour at least, especially if George asks him in
for a nightcap, as he probably will.' Rory's tone was calm
and bland. He held the door open, his pose loungingly
casual. 'Of course, you could knock his parents up, but it
is half past twelve and they'll have been asleep for several
hours. On a farm, people go to bed early and get up at
first light, or haven't you discovered that yet? I don't
think the Naughtons would be very happy about being
disturbed at this hour of the night.'

Zoe bit her lower lip, staring at him and unable to see a
flaw in his argument, although she strongly suspected he
was somehow tricking her.

'You're wet to the skin,' he drawled, running a
speculative eye over her. 'I thought I'd bring you here for
half an hour, give you a glass of brandy, let you dry out
and then drive you over to the farm in time to find Oliver
back home.'

Uncertainly, she asked, 'Is that what you told Oliver
you'd do?' Was he telling her the truth?

'You're shivering,' Rory said impatiently instead of
answering that. He reached into the car and caught hold
of her waist, pulling her out so suddenly that Zoe didn't

have time to decide what to do. She was half out of the car by the time she realised what he was intending and now that her wet clothes were beginning to dry on her she was shivering convulsively, so she didn't struggle any more. She got out and followed him through a side door into the house.

Rory took her along a slate-tiled corridor into a spacious sitting-room. As he switched on the electric light, she received an impression of warmth and colour. The curtains were a bold orange cotton and the carpet an olive green, the walls glowed with a creamy white paint and everywhere Rory had hung canvases of his own and work by other artists so that the eyes were assaulted by a vibrant life.

He moved over to switch on an electric fire. 'You'd better get out of those wet clothes!' he told her as he straightened, and Zoe stiffened.

'They're almost dry now!' she argued, but he walked towards her purposefully, took her arm in a punishing grip and forced her backwards to another door, ignoring her struggles.

'Let go, stop it, don't manhandle me like that,' Zoe muttered hoarsely, trying to hit him. 'What do you think you're doing?'

With his free hand he opened the door and pushed her through it. Her nervous eyes darted around, taking in the fact that she was in a bedroom. Pale and angry, she backed away from him, her eyes enormous and her body trembling.

'In that wardrobe over there you'll find some of my clothes. Take off that dress and put on a dressing-gown or one of my track-suits and I'll dry the dress in front of the fire.'

Zoe didn't move, her body like a ramrod as she waited to see what he meant to do next.

Rory eyed her with angry mockery. 'While you're doing that I'll make some hot coffee and you can have your brandy with it.' He gestured to the door with one casual wave. 'And there's a bolt on here,' he added before he went out.

She shot the bolt on the door the minute he was outside. She didn't care what he thought. She didn't trust him, not an inch. Only then did she strip off her dress and, still shivering, hunt through his wardrobe for something else to wear. She picked out a pale green terry-towelling jogging suit. It didn't fit very well, but she felt much warmer and safer when she had it on. She washed her face and hands in Rory's bathroom, which led out of the bedroom, combed her damp hair back into place and then went back into the sitting-room.

Rory was just carrying a tray into the room; steaming cups of coffee stood on it along with two glasses of brandy. He put the tray down on a table, coolly took Zoe's coral dress from her and vanished with it. She curled up on the carpet next to the electric fire and gratefully let the heat soak into her chilled body.

When he came back she asked, 'What have you done with my dress?' and he shrugged.

'It's drying in the kitchen in front of the Aga.' He brought her a cup of coffee and a glass of brandy and she set them down on the carpet next to her, then picked up the coffee again and curled her hands round it. Her pale fingers relaxed a little in the warmth of the hot liquid, and she inhaled the delicious smell of the coffee.

'Feel better?' asked Rory as he came over to sink into a deep black leather armchair, stretching his long legs out towards the fire.

'Yes, thank you.' Her voice was too husky; she looked away.

He had taken off his jacket and was wearing a thick black sweater with a roll neck. His hair had been brushed but was still damp, his lean face was relaxed, but Zoe felt uneasiness coiling in her stomach. This was too intimate, she was afraid of being alone with him.

The rain was still beating against the windows, the gutters ran with water, gurgling and splashing. The heat of the fire made her eyelids heavy, but her body throbbed with aroused pulses and her skin felt so sensitive that if he had touched it with the merest fingertip she would have cried out in shock.

'You aren't the way I expected you to be,' he said suddenly, taking her by surprise.

'What were you expecting?' she asked, curious until she began to see the danger of that avenue of talk.

'At seventeen you were amazingly adult,' he murmured softly, and all the little hairs on the back of her neck began to bristle. She remembered that tone vividly; the way his voice dropped, deepened, yet at the same time warmed and softened intimately. She had thought she would never hear it again and it sent her pulses haywire. She clamped her fingers around her cup and drank a little coffee to pull herself together.

'I suppose I thought you were going to stay the same but get older,' Rory went on, and her temper ran away with her.

'You expected me to stay crazy about you for the rest of my life, I suppose?' she snarled, then was immediately scarlet and unable to breathe with the shock of having been so stupid as to blurt that out. It was one thing to think it but another to admit to him what was in her mind. They both knew she had been wildly in love with him, but it had been safely in the past until she was stupid enough to open her mouth and mention it.

While she was still off balance Rory moved. One minute he was sitting in a chair some feet away, the next he was kneeling on the floor next to her, wicked mockery in his face.

'Are we going to stop playing games now?' he asked, taking her coffee-cup from her nerveless hands and putting it down on the mantelpiece out of reach, presumably in case she chucked it at him.

'I don't play games!' Zoe began to scramble to her feet, but he was too quick for her. He caught hold of her shoulders and pushed her backwards before she could free herself. A second later she was pinned on the carpet, her eyes darkening as she looked up at him.

'Don't you?' His mouth twisted and he smiled incredulously at her. 'Come on, Zoe, admit it. We both know why you came to Cumbria after you saw my exhibition, and it wasn't because you fell for Oliver Naughton. You came here to find me.'

She couldn't speak, her lips apart and dry, her blood racing so fast she could barely hear, either, the thunder in her ears deafening her. Even if she could have got a sound out what could she have said, anyway? He was right; it was true. She had come here to find him, although she had lied to herself because she couldn't bear to face the fact. Once she knew where he was she had needed to see him, she had had to come.

Rory's eyes were brilliant with excitement; she read that look and understood it all too clearly, and it made her shake in helpless response. He was bending down towards her; she watched his hard-featured face coming closer and closer as it had so many times in her dreams over the past seven years. She stared up at the grey eyes glittering with desire, the taut skin stretched over his angular bone-structure, the fierce sexual promise of that mouth—and knew she was reliving moments that had haunted her without mercy since he walked out on her, knew too that this was what she had come here for.

Seven years ago, he had planted a poisoned barb under her skin, which had tormented her ever since. It had to come out, but only Rory could cure her of wanting him; no other man could ever satisfy the frustrated need left inside her. Her eyes hated and desired him and she made no effort to evade the seeking of his mouth; her body arched towards him as if she were plastic yielding to the hot pressure of his hands. Her arms went round his neck, her eyes closed and she fell back into the recurring dream that had visited her bed night after night throughout the years since Provence, but this time she dreamt waking, able to control what happened, fully aware, as if she had split into two. One part of her moved hungrily in his arms, mindlessly kissing him, her fingers twining in his thick black hair, clasping the nape of his neck and stroking upwards to pull his head down closer. The other half of her had separated itself and hovered overhead, disembodied and cool-headed, watching in icy assessment.

This was what she had dreamt about all this time? She had locked up her heart and thrown away the key for this?

Her body was out of the deep-freeze and her senses rioted hotly but her mind never lost control, and when Rory's hands slid under the clinging top of the tracksuit she decided it was time to call a halt before things got out of hand.

He was too absorbed in his own excitement to realise that she was no longer responding. When she wriggled sideways and got up Rory's eyes snapped open in stunned surprise. He lay staring up at her, darkly flushed and breathing thickly, and Zoe coolly moved away while she ran a hand over her ruffled hair and smoothed down the track-suit top he had disarranged.

'Will you drive me back to the farm now, please?'

'What's wrong?' he asked disbelievingly.

'Nothing.' She made for the door to the kitchen. 'Do you mind if I borrow this track-suit? There's no point in changing back into my dress. I'll take it with me, though, and I'll have your track-suit washed and let you have it back tomorrow.'

'Damn the track-suit!' Rory muttered savagely, getting to his feet to follow her.

She found her dress hanging in front of the stove and pulled it down. Turning with the dress over her arm, she found Rory right in front of her, and her spine stiffened.

'You aren't going until I know what made you change your mind.' He told her through his teeth, his eyes probing the icy contours of her averted face.

'Let's just say I suddenly realised it didn't work,' she said offhandedly. 'I admit I did think I might still fancy you, but I found I was wrong, it was a silly mistake.'

'I don't believe you!' His voice was harsh and thick with rage. He didn't like being rejected any more than she had seven years ago. A little flare of satisfaction lit inside her, and then she felt worried because she didn't want to feel anything for him any more, even triumph in having escaped from caring about him.

'Look, I'm sorry,' she said. 'It's just one of those things. I didn't mean to lead you on, it just happened, and I don't see that there's any point in talking about it. I'm tired, and I'd like to go.'

'A minute ago you gave every impression of wanting me,' Rory said in a tone just a little short of a snarl. He was trying to keep his temper and not being very successful.

'I'm sorry,' she said again. 'I think I must have drunk too much at the barbecue.'

That made him angrier, his mouth hardened. 'Don't give me that! You're as sober as a judge!'

'I realise it must come as a shock to you,' Zoe retorted, 'but for once your irresistible charm has met an immovable object, so can we just forget it? Will you drive me back to the farm or must I walk?'

'What are you trying to do?' he asked, watching her with narrowed eyes. 'Get your own back? Zoe, seven years ago I . . .'

'I'm sick of talking about history,' she interrupted impatiently. 'Seven years ago I was just a kid, and what I did or thought or felt then has absolutely nothing to do with the present. When I let you kiss me just now it was because I was curious, I wondered how I *would* feel. Well, I didn't feel a thing.'

'Don't lie to me!' he erupted, glaring. 'I don't fool easily where women are concerned . . .'

'No,' she snapped. 'It's the women who get fooled, or rather the adolescents—because only someone young and naïve would be stupid enough to fall for your phoney line.'

Rory looked as if he didn't believe his ears, staring at her. Zoe laughed angrily at him.

'What's the matter? Did you think I couldn't see through you, even now? I may have been taken in seven years ago when I was as green as grass, and Lindy Ash may think you're the eighth wonder of the world, but any woman with two grains of sense would steer clear of you. I heard what you said to Lindy tonight, remember. "I've nearly finished with you," you said, and you didn't just mean as far as her portrait was concerned. For you, art and a love affair mean much the same thing. While you were painting me you gave a very convincing perform-ance of being in love and when you'd got bored with painting me you walked away without saying goodbye. That's how it will be with Lindy, won't it? I wonder if she's begun to guess already?' She gave him a malicious smile. 'I have a feeling Lindy isn't going to be quite so easy to walk away from, though. She may look like a little kitten, but she has sharp claws and she's dug them into you, run them in deep—she won't let you go so easily. You may have to move again. Is that what you always do? Move on? Leave the latest one behind?'

Rory still seemed to be lost for words, and when she stopped, out of breath and invective at the same time, they stared at each other in silence for what seemed a long time. He was looking at her as if he had never seen her before and she was wondering what he was thinking, but apparently he had no intention of telling her. He suddenly turned on his heel and walked out of the kitchen. Zoe slowly followed him along the shadowy corridor to the garage. He had climbed behind the wheel of his car. She got into the passenger seat just as the garage door rose electronically, and a moment later they were driving away at a speed which sent her heart into her mouth. Rory was in a black temper, taking corners on three wheels with a noise like Brands Hatch, and the lines of his face as sharp as if they had been incised with a razor.

Zoe wouldn't ask him to slow down; she wouldn't betray the state of her nerves as she clutched her hands together in her lap and turned her head sideways to watch the silver glitter of the sea on her left rather than the rush and roar of the seal-black wet road in front of them. The rain had stopped and the sky was clear and cloudless; moonlight trickled down through the trees and gave a dappled brightness to the village as they swept through it.

He pulled up outside the farmhouse, his tyres squealing, and Zoe gave him an angry look. 'I hope you're proud of that exhibition! Don't ever ask me to get into your car again.'

His hands tapped on the wheel. She thought he wasn't going to answer her and began to slide out of the seat, but just before she shut the door Rory said harshly, 'I don't know where you got the idea that I've ever made love to Lindy, but it isn't true. I haven't laid a finger on her.'

She gave him an incredulous look and slammed the door. Did he really expect her to believe that? She heard the full-throttled roar of his engine as she walked to the farmhouse door, and a moment later there was Oliver on the front doorstep, staring after Rory's tail lights with a frown.

'I was starting to get worried,' he told her as he held the door open for her to pass him. 'What happened to you? Where did he take you? Back to his house?' He caught sight of her face and his frown deepened. 'Are you okay, Zoe?'

'I'm tired, but I'm okay,' she said with a pretence of a smile. 'He told me you'd taken Lindy and her father home because their engine had flooded.' Her voice held a question mark.

'That's right, I did—you didn't mind, did you? He said he'd bring you back here. It didn't occur to me that he might hijack you.' Oliver closed the door, his voice low.

'He said your parents would be in bed and might not like being woken up.' She glanced up the stairs; all the lights were out up there.

He followed her along the hall and into the well-lit kitchen. 'But I told him my parents always left a key under the mat! I've often forgotten my front-door key in the past and had to knock them up, so they got into the habit of leaving a key outside for me. We don't have any trouble with burglars around here—we don't have anything worth stealing for a start, and anyway this is a very quiet country district. A stranger is always noticed and remembered.'

He was gabbling and staring oddly at her, and Zoe wondered why until she realised what had confused him. She had forgotten that she was wearing Rory's track-suit and carrying her coral-pink dress over her arm.

'It isn't quite as bad as it looks, Oliver,' she said drily, laying her dress over the back of a chair and smiling as Oliver turned distinctly red. 'I was caught in that rainstorm, and soaked to the skin, so when we got to his house he made me borrow this track-suit. That was as far as it went! I had a cup of coffee while my dress dried in front of his Aga. Nothing more spectacular than that, I'm afraid.'

'I didn't think ... of course, perfectly natural,' he stammered, and she eyed him wryly.

'You can stop tying yourself in knots! I'm sure it looked suspicious. Did Lindy know he was taking me home?'

He nodded. 'She was in a very sulky mood, I couldn't get a word out of her.'

'Poor kid,' said Zoe sighing. 'I mentioned her to him, by the way, and he got very angry and said that he'd never laid a finger on her. He almost convinced me, too.'

Oliver did not look reassured. 'Perhaps he's serious about her,' he said rather hopelessly.

She picked up her dress without answering. 'I'm dead on my feet,' she said. 'I must go to bed. Goodnight, Oliver.'

'I only want her to be happy,' he said pathetically, his brown eyes doglike and pleading, as if Zoe could make his world suddenly perfect if she only chose.

'Then save her from Rory Ormond,' she told him crisply, but Oliver was having second thoughts about the situation, his face uncertain as he followed her to the door, turning out the light.

'What if I'm wrong about him?'

'What on earth makes you think you are?' Zoe was

quite sure he wasn't, because if Rory had had any
genuine feelings for Lindy Ash he wouldn't have made
love to *her* that evening. Distaste made her mouth writhe.
He was a sexual opportunist and he didn't possess a
single decent impulse. He certainly didn't love her, but
he had made a strong pass at her and although he had
told her that he hadn't laid a finger on Lindy how could
you believe a word the man said? He'd hardly shown
himself to be someone you could rely on or believe!

'Well,' Oliver said helplessly, 'if he didn't make a pass
at you maybe he's in love with Lindy.'

Then she saw what he meant and grimaced. Oliver had
engineered what happened after the party so that she
should be alone with Rory Ormond in the hope that
something would happen between them!

'You mean you sent me off with him deliberately so
that he'd be tempted to make love to me?' she accused.

Oliver turned red, looking embarrassed and penitent.
'Well ... I ...' he mumbled, and she didn't know
whether to laugh or get angry with him. It was lucky
Oliver was so transparent; it meant she could always
guess what he was up to!

'You're not wrong about him!' Zoe assured him,
yawning, amused by the way Oliver's face lit up, even if
she didn't find it very funny to note the quick, eager,
curious look he sent her. Oliver was dying to know what
had happened tonight when she and Rory Ormond were
alone, but Zoe had no intention whatever of telling him a
thing.

'I'm going to bed!' she said, heading for the stairs, and
Oliver stumbled in her wake, whispering after her.

'Did he ... what ... you're sure?'

'Goodnight, Oliver,' she murmured, and a few minutes later was curled up in bed in the darkness, listening to the distant sound of the sea and feeling an identical restless surge in her own blood as she remembered how she had felt when Rory was kissing her. For a while she had almost lost her head and then the tide had ebbed away, leaving her beached and icy cold, full of bitter hostility to him after experiencing again the wild, head-spinning sweetness she had known in his arms seven years ago. Then he had taken her to the height of love, only to let her fall from it without warning; and she had wanted to kill him. She had been very young.

Now she felt very old, and she no longer wanted to kill him. She just wanted to hurt him, to cut him down to size, and if she could to make sure he didn't twist the heart of any other wide-eyed adolescent.

Well, tonight she had tasted triumph. She had drawn first blood. She stared up at the ceiling where moonlight moved like shallow water; silently gloating. His face! He had been so surprised, quite incredulous—she had turned him down! He couldn't believe it! He had been so sure of himself until then, convinced of his power over her.

While he was driving her back to the farm, she had told herself that she might as well go back to London in the morning. She had achieved what she had come here to do—she had broken the spell Rory Ormond had woven around her; the ice had cracked and she was free, she could feel her hot blood throbbing through her veins and her emotions flowing with the same heat. Never again would she need to back away from a man who tried to get close to her. She needn't be afraid of her own feelings or those of anyone else because what had happened tonight had proved to her that she could always control herself, rein in her feelings, handle whatever happened. She wasn't a vulnerable, defenceless girl any more. She was a sophisticated, self-aware woman and nobody was ever hurting her again, especially Rory Ormond.

But she had changed her mind about going back to London. She might have broken free of him—but there was still Lindy Ash to worry about and she had promised Oliver to do what she could for Lindy.

I must talk to her! Zoe thought, turning over and settling down to sleep. It wouldn't be a simple matter because Lindy didn't like her, was hostile to her; but once Lindy heard what Rory had done seven years ago wouldn't she realise she couldn't trust him?

If she's crazy about him, would she listen, though? Yawning, Zoe gave up thinking about it. She was really too tired to concentrate on anything tonight; she had to get some sleep.

She overslept next morning and when she got downstairs found Mrs Naughton pinning out washing in the strong sunshine. There was no sign of Oliver or his father. 'Hallo, did you sleep well?' Mrs Naughton greeted her, smiling cheerfully, and Zoe nodded.

'I'm afraid so—it's so quiet here, there was no early morning traffic to wake me up as it does in London.' She gave an apologetic smile.

'It probably did you good, then,' Mrs Naughton reassured her. 'I've managed to get all my washing done, so why don't I cook you some breakfast—what would you like? Bacon and egg? Sausages?'

'Oh, good heavens, it's nice of you, but I don't eat a

cooked breakfast. I'd love a slice of toast and some coffee, but I can get it myself, there's no need for you to do it. I don't want to make work for you.'

'Nonsense, sit down and I'll make your coffee. It isn't often I have a visitor to talk to while the men are working.'

'Where are they working?' Zoe stood by the window and stared into the farmyard but could see no sign of activity around the barns.

'They're up in the high pasture, mending a wall. They'll be back later, but they took some sandwiches so they won't be down for lunch. I promised Oliver I'd take you out to lunch. I thought we might run into Carlisle, do some shopping.' Mrs Naughton took the toast which had just popped up and put it on a plate. Zoe came to the deal table and sat down to eat the toast with some home-made marmalade which had a tangy taste and delicate curls of peel embedded in it. While she ate, and drank her coffee, Mrs Naughton sat down to talk to her cheerfully, asking her questions, confiding family news.

'It's very kind of you to have me here,' said Zoe during a lull in Mrs Naughton's chat, and the older woman shook her head, sunlight giving a bright silver gleam to her hair.

'I like having you. We don't have enough visitors. We lead such a quiet life, and that's how we prefer it, but it makes a nice change to have someone to stay. For one thing, you've given me a good excuse for going to Carlisle—it's really very close, yet we rarely go there. In the country it's easy to get into the habit of not bothering to go out. You've forced me out of my rut!'

'You seem to have lots of friends, though,' Zoe

remarked, and Mrs Naughton laughed.

'Oh, yes. In a small place people are much friendlier than they are in a city, I suppose. We have to get along together—if we didn't life would soon be unbearable.' She began to clear the table and Zoe helped her before running upstairs to get ready for the trip to Carlisle. She put on a thin linen jacket over her striped red and white shirt and white jeans, surveying her reflection briefly to make sure her hair was tidy and her make-up immaculate.

Carlisle was a very old city which had been extensively modernised over the past decade, and while Mrs Naughton shopped in The Lanes, a pedestrian-precinct shopping centre, Zoe visited the cathedral and the city museum before meeting Mrs Naughton again for lunch. They both had steak and salad followed by fruit salad. Zoe insited on buying a half-bottle of wine with the lunch, then they lingered over their black coffee for quite a while before they drove back to the farm.

As they passed the riding-stables Mrs Naughton slowed down. 'I'd like to call in and see how Maggie is,' she said, giving Zoe a questioning look. 'Would you mind? She may need some help with clearing up after her barbecue. A party always makes such a lot of work both before and afterwards.'

Of course Zoe said she didn't mind at all, she had liked Maggie and would be pleased to meet her again. Mrs Naughton parked on the drive which Zoe remembered only too well. A little shiver ran over her as they passed the place where Rory had picked her up last night. It looked very different in the daylight; the stone house and the barns and stable buildings were solidly down to earth without the romantic shadows and firelight to give them allure. The half-doors on the stalls had been flapped back; horses peered at them, snorting, as they walked round through the yard, over the straw-littered cobbles, to the back door.

Maggie heard them before they knocked. She looked out through a window and waved and a moment later smiled at them on the step of the kitchen.

'Come in and have a cup of tea! I haven't got any customers for half an hour and then it's only little Jackie Watson, who likes to practise going over the jumps on her own anyway. She's really good. She took two ribbons at the last gymkhana, but you remember, Olivia! I'd forgotten you were there, watching Oliver ride his hunter. He ought to have got that cup, Petrol is one of the best geldings in the district, but I don't think Oliver had his mind on what he was doing and the horse can't do it all.'

As she talked she had ushered them into a bright, sunny kitchen and put on the kettle. Zoe was stupidly surprised to hear that Oliver rode, but suddenly remembered noticing a large black horse in a field at the farm while Oliver was showing her around the previous day. Was that his hunter?

'Do you ride, Zoe?' asked Maggie, and Zoe shook her head, laughing.

'I'm afraid not. I did a little riding when I was at school, but it was so expensive that I gave it up. I enjoyed it very much, though. Now that I'm at work I suppose I could start again. There are stables in London.'

'Why not take out a horse while you're here?' Mrs Naughton suggested, and Maggie nodded.

'Yes, why don't you, Zoe? You can take your pick today—Jackie's pony would be too small for you, but I've got some quiet, well-behaved mounts for you to choose from. They won't give you any trouble.'

Zoe hesitated, tempted but a little nervous. It was a long time since she had been on a horse. 'Well, some time, perhaps . . .' she said, and Mrs Naughton gave her a teasing look.

'Scared? Maggie will take care you don't hurt yourself, and there's no time like the present. I'll leave you here to have a ride and Oliver can come and pick you up in a couple of hours.'

A tremor of panic went through Zoe at the thought of being plunged into riding at once. 'Oh, I don't think . . .' she stammered. 'I'm not dressed to go riding.'

'Jeans are fine,' Maggie said firmly. 'And I'll lend you some riding boots, your feet look as if they're my size! My hat should fit you too.' She turned to the stove to make the tea as the kettle boiled and Zoe stared blankly at her back, biting her lip.

Maggie began to pour the tea, then gave Zoe a quick, appraising look. 'Are you really bothered by the idea? Because if you are scared we'll just forget it. I don't want to push you into it because a horse always knows if you're frightened and plays up.'

Zoe met her frowning eyes and relaxed, grinning. 'Well, so long as I do get a nice quiet horse I would rather like to have a shot, actually.'

'Okay, then,' said Maggie, smiling back. 'And I'll be with you all the time, so there's no need to be nervous. If you have ridden before it will all come back to you, don't worry.'

Mrs Naughton drank her tea, looking rather amused. 'I've half a mind to stay and watch!'

'Oh, no, you don't,' Maggie told her. 'I know you, Olivia Naughton—you're hoping for some fun with a beginner! Zoe won't want an audience for her first ride.'

'No, I won't,' Zoe agreed vehemently, and they both laughed. Mrs Naughton left a short time later, after discovering that Maggie had already had the paddock cleared of all the debris from the barbecue, and Zoe tried on Maggie's hat and boots and found they fitted very well. She followed Maggie out into the yard and they inspected the quietest mounts in the stable. Zoe eventually picked out a gentle-eyed bay mare and Maggie saddled it for her.

'Does Lindy Ash ride?'

Maggie didn't lift her head; she went on tightening the girths and checking the height of the stirrups, standing close to the bay's warm body.

'Yes. I taught her years ago when she was about seven. She was rather a sweet little girl.'

'What changed her?' Zoe asked wryly, and Maggie laughed without much amusement.

'Oh, her mother's death, I suppose, and having her father all to herself. George over-compensated. He was so busy trying to make sure she didn't lose out in any way that he spoilt her. George is a very gentle man; it isn't in his nature to get tough with anyone, especially a little girl who's lost her mother!'

Zoe grimaced. 'No, I imagine it wasn't easy for him, bringing up a little girl all on his own. It's a pity she's so hard to like, though—she hardly goes out of her way to be friendly, does she? And it's even more obvious because everyone else around here is so nice and friendly.'

'Lindy never learnt to bother about other people,' Maggie said with a sigh. 'That's the whole trouble. She thinks the world revolves around her! Some day someone is going to give her the good slapping she deserves!'

Maggie's suddenly angry voice made Zoe stare, taken aback. It was out of character for Maggie to lose her temper or turn nasty, but her face was flushed and there was no doubt about it—Maggie was scowling.

'You sound as if you're really furious with her!' Zoe said slowly. 'What did she do to make you so mad?'

'Only ruin my chance of being happy,' Maggie said with bitterness. 'That spoilt little cat is deliberately getting between me and the man I love!'

Zoe's heart contracted painfully and she almost seemed to stop breathing. She stood there staring at Maggie's flushed profile, listening with a mixture of shock and dismay. So it was true! Maggie Thorn was in love with Rory and jealous of Lindy Ash! For once the gossips had hit the button; there was fire behind all that smoke.

NO COST! NO OBLIGATION!
NO PURCHASE NECESSARY!

PLAY "LUCKY 7"
AND GET AS MANY AS SIX FREE GIFTS...

HOW TO PLAY:

1. With a coin, carefully scratch off the three silver boxes at the right. This makes you eligible to receive one or more free books, and possibly other gifts, depending on what is revealed beneath the scratch-off area.

2. You'll receive brand-new Harlequin Presents® novels, never before published. When you return this card, we'll send you the books and gifts you qualify for absolutely free!

3. And, a month later, we'll send you 8 additional novels to read and enjoy. If you decide to keep them, you'll pay only $1.99 per book, a savings of 26¢ per book. There is no extra charge for postage and handling. There are no hidden extras.

4. We'll also send you additional free gifts from time to time, as well as our newsletter.

5. You must be completely satisfied, or you may return a shipment of books and cancel at any time.

DETACH AND MAIL CARD TODAY

BUSINESS REPLY CARD

First Class   Permit No. 717   Buffalo, NY

Postage will be paid by addressee

Harlequin Reader Service®
901 Fuhrmann Blvd.,
P.O. Box 1867
Buffalo, NY 14240-9952

NO POSTAGE
NECESSARY
IF MAILED
IN THE
UNITED STATES

CHAPTER FIVE

WHEN Oliver picked Zoe up a couple of hours later, she was glowing with satisfaction because she had remembered skills she thought she had long forgotten; it had all come flooding back as soon as she was on the horse's back and walking the mare around the little paddock. Within half an hour she had been cantering and taking low jumps and Maggie had grinned approval, clapping her, from the gate. Zoe hadn't gone on riding for too long; she didn't want an aching set of muscles tomorrow, so she had climbed off the mare not long before Oliver arrived, and she and Maggie had unsaddled the bay and put her back into her stable, then gone to have a cup of tea.

They had talked lightly while they waited for Oliver. Zoe hadn't mentioned Rory; it had not seemed tactful, but, more than that, she couldn't bear to talk to Maggie about him. She had kept on the safe subject of the Cumbrian landscape and the history of the area. This was Maggie's passion; she was always glad to talk about that, but her mind kept straying in one direction and Zoe had to keep gently leading her back.

'George does some fascinating maps of Cumbria,' Maggie said at one point. 'At places like Hadrian's Wall, for instance, he does drawings of Roman life there; fights with the Picts or trading with the British. The history teacher at his school puts them on the wall and uses them in lessons. George is very clever.'

'He's nice, too. I like him,' Zoe said warmly, and Maggie gave her a wry look, pulling a face.

'Well, sometimes I admit I feel like beating his head on a wall. He's as blind as a bat, in some ways—his daughter, for instance! He just can't see what she's up to; he doesn't understand her. He had the idea of Rory painting Lindy, and now . . .' Maggie broke off as there was a tap on the back door. 'Come in!' she called, and Oliver appeared, smiling at them both.

'How did the riding lesson go?' he asked, and Maggie assured him that Zoe had been a good pupil.

'She's a natural rider,' she added, and Zoe flushed with pleasure, shaking her head.

'I'm nothing of the kind!'

'You picked it all up again in minutes,' Maggie insisted. 'How do you feel about coming over for a ride tomorrow, Oliver? To keep Zoe company?'

'Love to,' he said casually, and got a grateful smile from Zoe.

On the way back to the farm, Oliver suddenly said, 'George Ash rang and invited us over there for supper— how do you feel about going? I said we would go, but I can always ring up and say you're feeling too tired after your riding lesson.'

Zoe froze in her seat, thinking hard. 'No, I'd like to go,' she said slowly, and Oliver lit up.

'Great. Lindy's cooking a hotpot.' He laughed suddenly. 'Goodness knows what it'll be like! I didn't even know she could cook!'

'What should I wear?' asked Zoe as they arrived back at the farmhouse, and Oliver shrugged indifferently.

'Nothing special, not for supper with George and Lindy! I'll wear jeans and a shirt.'

'Then so will I,' Zoe said, but knew she would take some trouble to make sure she looked very good in her jeans and shirt because she was not letting Lindy Ash outshine her.

'How do you feel?' asked Mrs Naughton, meeting her in the hall, and Zoe pulled a droll face.

'I know where every one of my muscles is, anyway!'

Mrs Naughton laughed. 'It'll be worse tomorrow! Were you thrown?'

'No, the mare was very patient and gentle!'

'Maggie says she's very good,' Oliver told his mother, joining them after parking the car. 'Take no notice of Zoe; she's just being modest.'

'I suspected as much,' said Mrs Naughton, smiling at Zoe, who wryly shook her head.

'I was lucky to have a good teacher and a well-behaved horse,' she insisted. 'But I'd love a long, hot bath, all the same! I'm not used to this exercise!'

There were chuckles from mother and son and Mrs Naughton waved a hand up the stairs. 'Off you go, then! The water's hot.'

Zoe closed the bathroom door and locked it with a sigh of relief. She needed to be alone for a while. She hadn't had a chance to think properly all day and her mind had been seething with a confusion of realisations and feelings that had to be sorted out. She began to run her bath and then stripped, biting her lip as she remembered Maggie's face when she talked about Lindy Ash coming between her and the man she loved. Maggie had looked so unhappy; her eyes shining with unshed tears and her face first pale and then dark red. Zoe had felt instinctive pity for her, and yet at the same time she had felt that sharp stab between her ribs. She refused to call it either pain or rage—but it hadn't been pleasant, and she was angry just remembering it.

Rory Ormond should be shot! she thought, climbing into the foaming bathwater a moment later and lying down with a long sigh of pleasure as her weary muscles gratefully relaxed in the warmth. He was far too shrewd and aware not to know that Maggie was in love with him. Had he dated Maggie until Lindy came on the scene?

Her body stiffened in the scented water, her eyes shutting in a reflex of pain. Were he and Maggie lovers, had they slept with each other?

The very idea made her feel ill, and that appalled her, because how could she go on telling herself how indifferent she was to him, when she was jealous of his relationships with other women?

She tried to comfort herself with the idea that her jealousy was merely a habit; something she couldn't throw off but which she had long ago outgrown. It sounded good, but Zoe couldn't quite convince herself, because the jabs of jealousy were far too real.

She took her time over her bath and then padded into her bedroom in a short towelling robe to get dressed for supper with George and Lindy Ash. Why had Lindy invited them? Zoe pondered as she slid into smooth blue jeans and a blue and white striped shirt. Her reflection threw back an image of cool control; she wished she felt the way she looked. At least she wouldn't have to see Rory tonight. If he had been invited, Oliver would have mentioned it, and he wouldn't have looked so cheerful.

'You look fabulous,' Oliver told her when he saw her later.

'Thank you,' she said demurely. 'You look nice, too.' He was in jeans, as he had promised, and was wearing a

red check shirt with an open neck and no tie. He looked
fresh and healthy, as usual, his fair hair faintly damp
after the shower he had taken when Zoe finally vacated
the bathroom.

He looked pleased by her compliment and ran a hand
over his well-brushed hair. 'I ought to buy some new
clothes, I suppose. I only ever wear jeans and shirts and
on the farm that doesn't matter. No point in wearing
anything else. But maybe I ought to get a few good suits.'

He didn't add: to impress Lindy! but Zoe read the
unspoken words in his eyes and her mouth twisted
impatiently. Too many people thought too much about
Lindy Ash. No wonder she was spoilt and arrogant! No
doubt she thought the whole world revolved around her;
and as far as some people were concerned it apparently
did. You could understand her father being devoted to
his only child, but Lindy dominated the lives of Maggie
Thorn and the Naughtons too—not to mention Rory
Ormond.

That reminded her that she hadn't asked Oliver if they
were to be the only guests at the supper, so she made a
casual enquiry and saw Oliver's face fall.

'They didn't say. You don't think *he's* likely to be there
too?'

Zoe didn't need to ask who 'he' meant—the name lay
between them like an unexploded bomb and they skirted
it warily.

'I just wondered!' she said.

'I hope not!' Oliver muttered glumly. Zoe didn't admit
that she hoped not too, but their eyes met and exchanged
the rueful thought.

George Ash had a small, white-painted cottage built of
local stone some time in the nineteenth century. It had

been modernised by having a dormer window thrown out through the steeply pitched roof, giving another room on the upper floor. There was only a small garden in front of the cottage, and Oliver parked on the narrow lane in a parking place a short walk from the wooden gate, at which he first dropped Zoe. She didn't feel like facing Lindy Ash yet, so she waited for Oliver to join her, hovering on the paved path staring at the glorious confusion of an English cottage garden in summer riot; spires of delphiniums and hollyhocks backing carnations and roses and sweet williams and pansies. The colour was vivid and the air heavy with scent and the hum of bees still foraging before dusk fell. Zoe felt a wave of melancholy sweep over her. The scene was so peaceful, but she was far from being at peace; she was as muddled as the flowers growing cheek by jowl.

The front door opened and her eyes flicked towards it warily, dilating as she saw Rory framed there.

'Are you coming in or not?' he asked, lifting one black brow.

'I was waiting for Oliver.' Her voice was husky, which irritated her. When was she going to be able to look at him without this immediate shock and confusion? 'Are you having supper too?' she asked without moving towards him, and Rory came down the path towards her.

'Yes—don't sound too pleased, will you?' The ironic glint in his eyes made her teeth meet, and she looked behind her in search of Oliver. What on earth was he doing all this time? He only had to park the car and walk back to the cottage!

'What a pretty garden!' she said, to keep the talk on an impersonal level.

It didn't fool Rory; his mouth twisted and his eyes

mocked her. 'Isn't it? George is a passionate gardener, he loves colour, of course, and gardening is another sort of art.' He bent and picked a white rose which he coolly inserted into Zoe's short, dark hair, just above her ear. Her spine stiffened and her blood flowed hotly into her face as she felt his fingers moving on her hair, against her skin. Rory lounged next to her, assessing the effect of the soft-petalled flower on the way she looked. His eyes were half-hooded, glinting.

'I'd like to paint you in a garden,' he thought aloud. 'Lying among white roses and lilies—I could get some interesting reflections on your skin.'

'Oh, no, you won't!' she muttered, angrily pulling the rose out of her hair, ignoring the tugged strands which came with it. She threw it at Rory, who caught it instinctively, by the stem, then gave a sharp exclamation.

'Hell!' He lifted his finger and sucked at it, eyeing her broodingly. 'I've got a thorn in my finger now!'

'Serves you right!' she said childishly and that made him laugh.

He held out his finger. 'Aren't you going to kiss it better?'

Zoe stared drily at him without either moving or replying and he grinned, threading the white rose into a buttonhole on his shirt.

'Thank you for the flower, anyway,' he drawled, as though she had given it to him instead of the other way around, then his eyes flicked past her and he said, 'Oh, hallo, Naughton!' his voice flat.

'Hallo,' Oliver returned with the same lack of enthusiasm. Zoe met Oliver's eyes and smiled ruefully.

'I wondered where you'd got to!' she said, and he sighed.

'I've got a puncture—there was some glass on the road further along and my tyre has gone completely flat. I'll have to change the wheel before we can go home.'

'Tough luck, said Rory with unhidden amusement, and Oliver glared at him.

'Where are George and Lindy?' Zoe asked quickly.

'In the kitchen checking on the hotpot. Lindy's a bit flustered because she's never cooked it before.' Rory let Oliver walk ahead and fell behind with her. 'I hear you went riding today.'

She shot him a frowning look. 'Maggie told you, I suppose?'

'No, it was George who mentioned it. I haven't talked to Maggie today.'

She watched his face intently and wished she could pierce the bland mask he was showing her. What went on inside that head of his? He had mentioned Maggie without a flicker of awareness; not a tremor had crossed his face, she might have been a complete stranger or a very distant acquaintance. You wouldn't guess she meant a thing to him.

'Maggie's nice,' she said carefully, and the grey eyes did slide towards her, then, narrowed and thoughtful.

'So she is!'

'I like her,' Zoe said, and his cool face glinted with wry amusement, especially as she flushed.

'Well, that's good. So do I.' He was mocking her, his face shrewd and speculative. Oliver had vanished into the house and was no doubt in the kitchen by now, with George and Lindy Ash. Zoe halted in the small hall and stared uncertainly around, wondering which way to turn.

Several doors stood open, and while she hesitated Rory gestured with one hand towards a door on the left.

'In here.'

She found herself in a sitting-room crowded with books and pictures; it was shabby and comfortable, and she wandered around, touching a small statuette here, a book there, absorbing something of George Ash's taste and character from his possessions. It wasn't hard to guess that Lindy hadn't contributed much to this room; Zoe couldn't imagine her choosing anything in it. But no doubt she had decorated her own room in the house and kept her books and records there.

'Why the character reference for Maggie Thorn?' Rory asked her abruptly, and she started, looking at him uneasily. She wished she hadn't mentioned Maggie now, but at the time she had been trying to prove to herself, as much as Rory, that she wasn't jealous of Maggie.

'Shouldn't we find the others? I could give Lindy a hand,' she said. It made her very nervous to be alone with him—even in a house full of other people.

'Why?' he demanded, then walked over to a table cluttered with bottles. 'I'm going to have a whisky—what can I get you?'

'I don't want anything, thanks.'

'George will be offended if you don't have a glass in your hand,' Rory said coolly, and filled a glass with orange juice which he spiked with a short dash of gin. 'Try this,' he said, putting the glass into her hand.

'Thank you,' Zoe said coldly, and put the glass down. 'What made you move up here?' she asked him, and he shrugged.

'I like the landscape. I lived in London for a while, but I don't like cities. My family came from up here—my grandfather farmed in the Borders and I had an uncle in the Lake District. So I knew the countryside very well and I felt that this was where I wanted to settle down when I stopped travelling around Europe.'

He was sipping his whisky and watching her intently over the rim of the glass, and she moved away nervously. She wished he wouldn't stare at her like that. Intent on keeping the talk light, she asked, 'When did you travel around Europe?'

'After I'd said goodbye to you,' he said very quietly, and she swung to face him, bitterness darkening her eyes.

'I don't remember you saying anything of the sort! You just vanished one day without a word.'

'It seemed the easiest way!' he said, and she laughed angrily, her eyes despising him.

'I'm sure it was—for you. After all, I might have been a nuisance, mightn't I? I might have cried or made a fuss and you wouldn't want that. It isn't your style. You wouldn't know how to handle a real emotion.'

Rory put down his glass and moved and she stepped behind a chair, shaking with rage.

'Don't come near me! I couldn't bear it if you touched me!'

He came to a stop a few feet away, his face stiff and hard. 'Listen to me, Zoe . . .'

'I listened to you seven years ago,' she interrupted hoarsely. 'We both know where that got me! I've no intention of ever listening to you again. I don't want to hear any more lies and fairy tales, so don't bother to feed me whatever clever story you've come up with to explain why you just walked out on me in Provence.' Her voice cut out suddenly as she heard voices outside the room. She turned hurriedly and stared out of the window into the garden, her eyes burning and fixed. Birds flew and called in the twilight; their notes melancholy as the shadows thickened around them and lights sprang up in the nearby village. The moon was moving softly up the sky; through glass the shimmer of the light blurred—or was she seeing it through unshed tears?

Behind her she heard Oliver and George Ash talking cheerfully to Rory. 'Supper won't be long now. Lindy just turned the oven up and that should brown the potato on the top of the hotpot.'

'Where's Zoe?' asked Oliver. 'Oh, there she is by the window!'

She blinked to force back the threat of tears and swallowed hard before turning to face the room.

'Hallo, George!' The bright smile pinned to her mouth didn't feel very convincing, but he smiled back without appearing to notice. 'It was nice of you to invite me tonight,' Zoe said warmly, thinking how much she liked him.

'It's a pleasure,' he said, as if he really meant it and wasn't merely making a polite reply. 'Let me get you a drink—Rory, you're a fine host, you didn't give Zoe a drink!'

'I did,' Rory said shortly, staring at Zoe, who tried to pretend she wasn't aware of those insistent eyes.

'I put it down somewhere.' She looked around and saw her glass. 'Oh, here it is!' She put out a hand to pick it up at exactly the same moment as Rory reached for it. She snatched her fingers away before he could touch them. It was a violent, involuntary reaction and she felt an answering violence in Rory, even though she was not looking at him. He let his hand fall and Zoe almost snatched her glass. Turning, she found herself faced with

Lindy who was standing in the doorway, watching them, her small face suffused with angry colour.

It was obvious that she had seen that brief, betraying scene and even more obvious that she didn't like what she had seen.

'There you are, darling!' said George Ash, blissfully unaware of the atmosphere in the room. 'Come and have a drink. How's the hotpot coming along?'

'It's fine,' said Lindy through her clenched teeth, and she swayed over to Rory's side to push her hand through his arm, clinging to him possessively. 'What are you drinking, Rory? I'll have one of those.'

'You won't,' Rory said shortly. 'This is whisky. I'll give you what I gave Zoe, orange with a dash of gin.'

Lindy scowled. 'I'm not still at school, you know!' She grasped his whisky and swallowed some, suppressing the little shudder she couldn't quite hide. Rory grinned at her, shaking his head.

'Do you want me to put you over my knee?' He firmly removed the glass and she giggled.

'Promises, promises!' she chanted, bright-eyed and defiant.

'If you like, you can have a glass of the red wine we've opened for supper,' he offered, and she followed him out of the room to find the wine. Zoe didn't glance after them; she stared, frowning, into the darkening garden in a mood of disturbed uneasiness. Watching Lindy a moment ago she had felt sorry for her.

George was frowning too; she saw his reflected face in the window and turned to look at him. He gave her a quick grimace. 'I'm not being a very good host, am I? Sorry. I'm worried about Lindy.'

Oliver's attention quickened and he exchanged looks

with Zoe, saying, 'What about Lindy, George? Anything wrong?'

George drank a little whisky, held his glass and stared into the amber liquid, his face rueful. 'She's going through a difficult patch—girl into woman, I suppose. Not an easy transition.'

'Rory Ormond's right out of her league, too,' Oliver said aggressively, and George looked at him in surprise.

'Rory? Oh, Rory's okay. I trust him with her. She won't come to any harm with him.'

Zoe couldn't help laughing shortly, and George turned his head to stare at her blankly.

'George, you're all wrong about Ormond,' said Oliver. 'Ask Zoe about the sort of man he is! Ask her if you can trust Ormond with Lindy.'

George slowly swivelled his head to gaze at Zoe; he didn't say anything, but his face was embarrassed and uneasy, and she felt herself flushing hotly. If she had ever had any doubts about whether George realised what sort of relationship she had had with Rory Ormond seven years ago, they were dispelled at that instant. George knew there had been a love affair and he was horrified by Oliver's attempt to talk about it. He didn't want to upset her, he was sorry for her.

That meant that he knew what sort of man Rory Ormond was—and Zoe was incredulous. Why, then, was George encouraging his own daughter to see so much of Rory, spend so much time alone with him? Surely he hadn't been naïve enough to imagine that his daughter, at least, would be taboo because Rory was his friend?

Angrily, Zoe burst out, 'You can't trust Rory Ormond with any woman!'

Oliver looked satisfied; George gaped at her, his

mouth wide open in an audible intake of air, and that was the moment when Rory and Lindy chose to come back. Zoe's harsh words seemed to hang on the air, reverberating. When she heard the movement by the door her eyes flashed across the room and met Rory's savage glare. She had never seen a look like that on his face before—he was so angry that his skin was suddenly white, pulled tightly over his cheekbones, which were thrust into prominence making his whole face look different; angles as sharp as a knife-edge and a mouth which was a physical threat, hard and straight and clamped together.

It was George who broke the silence, his voice thick with distressed embarrassment.

'I'm sure the supper's ready, Lindy, let's go and serve it up before it's ruined.' He bustled across the room and took his daughter's arm to thrust her out. Lindy didn't want to go; she struggled and began to protest, but her father insisted on removing her and Oliver followed them a moment later, his red face and averted eyes making it obvious that the tense atmosphere was driving him out too.

Zoe was frozen, her wide, dilated eyes held by Rory's. She was only just aware of the others retreating; all her attention was given to the grim threat in Rory's face.

It was only when he took a step towards her that the spell broke and she could move. Panic-stricken and trembling, she turned and fled from the room. She couldn't join the others in the kitchen; the very sound of their voices made her feel worse so she went along the narrow hallway out of the front door into the summer night, and that was a stupid mistake; she knew that even as she stumbled over the threshold and found herself in warm, breathing darkness. With the light doused, the gentle, domesticated landscape had changed—she stood on the path, trembling like someone confronting a loosed tiger, aware of danger in the night. The black outline of the hills, the smothering deep purple of the sky, pressed in upon her and her panic grew.

She would have run back into the house and risked facing the others, but Rory was behind her now.

She didn't need to look back and she hadn't heard him coming, yet she felt him there and her whole body went into acute shock; she couldn't breathe, she was icy cold and feverish at the same time, she was shaking violently and couldn't stop it.

She began to run without knowing where she was running to, and Rory was right behind her all the time. She kept expecting to feel his hands reach out for her; her skin dreaded his touch and craved it, and the stupidity of her own reactions to him made her so angry that she suddenly stopped dead and turned to face him.

'Why don't you leave me alone?' she broke out hoarsely, and he ignored her, his hands fastening on her shoulders so tightly that she cried out in pain.

'What the hell were you saying about me in there? What had you told George Ash to make him look at me like that?'

'I warned him not to trust you,' Zoe threw at him, watching the white blaze in his face with a painful satisfaction. His hands dug into her flesh, he shook her so violently that her head flew back and forth like the head of a rag doll shaken by a child, her short silky hair flying around in a swirl which brushed his face, strands whipped across his mouth. She felt his lips against her hair and looked up at him through the drifting, floating strands, her eyes enormous and dazed.

Rory stared back; she heard the harsh intake of his breath, then his mouth crushed down on hers and desire overwhelmed her. One minute she was straining to break free of him, the next their bodies collided in a feverish impact like the crash of stars on the edge of the universe; wild fire and the shattering of everything stable followed by darkness, smothering and velvety, the sense of being free from gravity, flying through space.

I'm delirious, Zoe thought, drowning in physical sensations she couldn't control, her hands moving restlessly, urgently, touching him with a driving need she had felt ever since she saw him again but which she still hated to admit. She couldn't understand why she couldn't stop feeling like this; her mind seemed to have no influence over her body at all.

She knew precisely what sort of man Rory Ormond was; why was she in his arms again, giving him kiss for kiss, caress for caress?

They both heard Lindy calling. 'Rory! Rory, where are you?' Her voice was high and wild with temper. She must have followed them out of the front door and be standing on the path, peering into the shadowy depths of the dark garden. She couldn't see them because Rory had caught Zoe under a willow whose long, trailing branches hid them and made a whispering green tent around them.

Rory slowly lifted his mouth, his face a pale blur above Zoe; glittering grey eyes raking over her uplifted features as she shuddered breathlessly, so weak that she had to lean back on the trunk of the willow. She wished she could hide her face from him; it was dangerous to let him see what he had done to her, but she couldn't look away or run, she was barely able to stand.

'Rory!' Lindy shouted again, nearer. She was walking

along the path; she might at any moment see the white gleam of Rory's shirt through the branches of the willow.

Zoe closed her eyes, her hands dropping to her sides. She didn't care if Lindy did see them. Wasn't that why she had come here? To make sure he didn't hurt another girl the way he had hurt her?

'Maybe now you'll listen to me,' Rory said thickly, his voice very low. 'You've got me all wrong, Zoe.'

Smiling bitterly, she shook her head very slowly, moving it from side to side in a tranced, rolling movement as though having started she couldn't stop.

'Oh, no,' she whispered, 'I haven't got you wrong. I know you very well.'

'You don't know me at all if you think I meant to hurt you,' he said sharply.

He had spoken too loudly; Lindy had heard him. 'Rory? What are you doing?' she asked furiously, hurrying in their direction, and Zoe began to laugh.

It wasn't amusement at all, of course; it was hysteria, and she couldn't stop the deep, choking noise even when she put a shaking hand over her mouth. Rory gave her a brief, harsh look and then he left her, pushing his way through the willow branches to meet Lindy, who as soon as she saw him broke out with high-pitched reproaches.

'Why are you out here? What's going on? Where's that girl? What are you doing?'

Her voice began to move further away, Zoe heard scuffling sounds; the grate of shoes on gravel, the rustle of Lindy's dress and over all that the girl's protests.

'I want to know what's been going on, why did you and that girl come out into the garden?'

She sounded intolerably young, childishly cross and jealous. Zoe kept her eyes shut, but that didn't stop the hot tears oozing between her lashes and down her cheeks. She despised herself; he had humiliated her again, and she hadn't done a thing to stop him, she had surrendered herself recklessly, and now she could hear that girl going through the same process she had gone through herself seven years before—helplessly in love and helplessly vulnerable.

She waited until they had gone into the house before she moved. She found a handkerchief in the pocket of her jeans and roughly dried her face; her make-up must be in a pitiful state, but there was nothing much she could do about that.

It wasn't going to be easy to go back into George Ash's house and face them all, but what else could she do? She combed her hair with her fingers and bit her lips to give them a little more colour, then walked through the clinging leafy branches just as Oliver came to find her.

He looked at her with sombre uncertainty, trying to seem normal. 'The supper's ready now,' he offered, and Zoe nodded.

'I'm coming.' On the path in the light from the house she halted and turned up her face. 'Do I look okay?'

Oliver was reluctant to look, but he politely did and nodded, then produced a comb and held it out. She ran it through her hair and gave it back.

'Thanks. Maybe we've got through to George Ash at last, anyway.' Her wry little smile was not too convincing, but Oliver smiled back gratefully.

'I'm sorry if . . . I hope you aren't too upset, Zoe. I didn't mean you to get hurt, it didn't enter my head that you might . . . well . . .'

His mumbling didn't make sense for a few seconds, then she realised what he was trying to say and flushed, grimacing. Oliver had finally guessed that she was not quite as indifferent to Rory Ormond as he had expected her to be, and he was sorry for her.

That was all she needed! Anger stiffened her backbone and she shrugged, her colour very high. She could do without Oliver's pity just as she could do without Rory Ormond; her self-respect made her resist both.

'Shall we go and eat this famous hotpot?' she asked crisply. 'It's probably burnt black by now.'

The last thing she wanted to do was eat, especially eat something Lindy Ash had cooked and over which so much fuss had been made, but she lifted her head defiantly and she and Oliver entered the house.

CHAPTER SIX

'YOU could be quite a good horsewoman if you worked at it,' Maggie told Zoe next day as they led the bay mare back to her stable after Zoe's lesson. 'You ride naturally, and that's something you can't buy or learn, it's a gift from heaven. A pity to waste it.'

Zoe leaned over the stable door watching Maggie working on the mare's sweating coat. It was very hot and Zoe was damp with sweat too, her shirt clung to her body and her hair felt almost wet.

'Did you enjoy supper with George last night?' Maggie asked casually, and her nerves jumped. She couldn't get a word out, the memory of the two hours spent in that house after she and Oliver walked back in from the garden had been hanging around in the back of her mind all day. She had refused to think about it. It had been a nightmare. All she wanted now was to forget it and on the way back to the farm she had told Oliver that she was returning to London.

It said a good deal for Oliver's new realisation of the situation that he hadn't argued, simply nodded.

'If you can wait until Dad and I have finished rebuilding that wall, I'll drive you back,' he had said quietly. 'Say the day after tomorrow? Is that okay?'

She had agreed, although she would much rather have gone this morning. She was afraid of seeing Rory again. There had been something in his eyes last night, as they sat on opposite sides of the supper-table, which had not

116

merely disturbed her. It had kept her awake half the night and as soon as she got up she had eaten a rapid breakfast and then accompanied Oliver and Mr Naughton up the hill to watch them working on the dry-stone wall which needed repair. They told her it was like the Forth Bridge; an unending task, no sooner had they repaired one stretch than another crumbled under rain or wind and they were back at work on it again. They had showed Zoe how they chose stones and set them in place and shaped them with chisel and hammer, and Zoe had helped, sorting out stones of the right size and shape for them.

'This is very dull for you,' Mr Naughton had protested. 'Why not let my wife take you for a drive to the Lakes?'

'Well, I promised to be at the stables at two,' she had said, and shortly after that she had gone back to the farm for a salad lunch with Mrs Naughton before setting out to walk to the stables over the fields, refusing a lift because she wanted to explore, on foot.

Maggie had finished grooming the horse; she shut the door and faced Zoe, her eyes curious.

'You didn't answer—didn't you enjoy Lindy's hotpot, or something?'

Zoe made a face. 'It was very good, actually.'

'But?' Maggie asked shrewdly, watching her.

'Oh, nothing,' Zoe evaded, walking away towards the house. 'Did you say something about making some tea? I'm as dry as a bone.'

'I've got some homemade lemonade in the fridge,' Maggie offered.

'Delicious, I'd love some, thank you.'

Zoe sat down in the comfortable kitchen with a sigh, massaging the back of her neck with one hand. 'All this exercise is very tiring.'

Maggie poured a glass of the chilled lemonade and delicately floated a thin slice of lemon on the top before handing it to her.

She sat down with her own glass and kicked off her boots, wiggling her feet in their white socks.

'George muttered something about Lindy making trouble,' she said lightly, then took a little sip of her lemonade and sighed. 'Umm, it is good—try it.'

Zoe drank some, closed her eyes and moaned. 'Oh, I'm so thirsty, I could drink the whole jugful. What's in it?'

'Lemons, sugar and a tiny dash of white wine.' Maggie grinned as Zoe's eyes opened in surprise. 'Well, why not? It gives a distinctive flavour.' She watched her take another drink, then said drily, 'Lindy's favourite occupation is making trouble. I wasn't surprised to hear she ruined the evening. George was rather mysterious, he seemed embarrassed—did Lindy say bitchy things to you, or would you rather not repeat what she said?'

Zoe sighed; there was rather more than a dash of wine in the lemonade, she suspected, because her head was beginning to feel a little cloudy, but it was a pleasant sensation, so she let Maggie refill her glass and drank some more, tempted to confide in Maggie even though she knew it was reckless.

'She wasn't exactly friendly, no! I can't help feeling sorry for her, all the same. She reminds me of a bird that's been trapped in a room with closed windows—she flutters around smashing into things, trying to find a way out, and doesn't seem to know what she's doing.'

Maggie frowned, her legs flung over the arm of her chair and her thin body relaxed although her face was far from being at ease. She stared at Zoe, hesitating.

'I'd have said she knew exactly what she was doing,' she said slowly. 'She wants to stop her father marrying again.'

Zoe's eyes snapped wide open. Amazed, she asked, 'Why on earth should she think that was likely?'

'George is only just forty,' Maggie said sharply. 'Why on earth shouldn't he marry again?'

Baffled, Zoe shrugged. 'Well, no reason why not, of course, but why should you think Lindy suspects he's interested in me?' Then her eyes rounded incredulously and she stared at Maggie with her mouth open. 'George hasn't hinted that he . . . surely not! Why, I've hardly exchanged two words with the man!'

'Not you,' said Maggie, very flushed and laughing wildly, 'I didn't mean you, for heaven's sake, it never crossed my mind.'

'Oh,' said Zoe, the penny dropping at last and she began to giggle too. 'I'm sorry, Maggie, I *must* be dumb!'

'Well, you said it,' Maggie said, still laughing, and as pink as one of the wild roses growing around her door.

She looked like a very young woman suddenly and Zoe blurted out, 'But everyone thinks that you're in love with . . .' She stopped, confused and realising she couldn't finish that sentence as it sank in that the gossip was way off course.

'With?' queried Maggie, looking puzzled and curious.

'I wonder what made them think that?' Zoe thought aloud. Had they noticed a new look in Maggie's eyes and hunted around for a man to explain the change? George had lived here for years, they wouldn't suspect him, would they? They would immediately fix on the newcomer in the neighbourhood; an attractive man of the right age and the allure of being famous and eligible into the bargain.

'You're maddening, do you know that?' said Maggie finishing her lemonade and pouring herself some more. 'Tell me, for heaven's sake, before I explode!'

'Oh, it doesn't matter,' Zoe hurriedly told her. 'Tell me about you and George.'

'It does matter! If everyone's been talking about me I want to know what they've been saying—and who is everyone, anyway? Who told you this? Mrs Naughton? She's never said a word to me.' Maggie stopped dead, staring at nothing. 'No, now I think about it—she has made the odd strange remark. I didn't take much notice at the time, but . . .' She focused on Zoe. 'Rory. It's Rory, isn't it?'

Zoe nodded, watching her, and Maggie began to laugh again.

'Me and Rory? They're out of their minds! What on earth put that idea into their heads? Wait until I see Olivia Naughton—I'll tease her silly over this and . . .' She stopped laughing and frowned. 'I wonder if Rory knows what they're all saying?'

'I don't suppose they would openly mention it to him,' Zoe thought aloud, and Maggie made a wry little face.

'They'd be sorry if they did! Rory doesn't pull his punches; if there's one thing that really puts him in a temper it's silly gossip of this type.' Maggie's frown deepened. 'As long as they haven't said anything to George!'

'Surely he would have mentioned it if they had!' Zoe protested, and Maggie looked at her uncertainly.

'George isn't very sure of himself. He's got a massive inferiority complex, and having Rory Ormond move into the district hasn't helped. George thinks the man is a great genius; by comparison with Rory, he feels insignificant. Any confidence he did have has been draining away ever since Rory turned up here. I like Rory, but I admit I wish he'd never come here.'

Zoe was bewildered now. Maggie had said she was in love with George and was thinking of marrying him, but it wasn't clear whether George had actually asked her, or even if their relationship was yet serious.

'You said Lindy didn't want her father to marry again,' she murmured tentatively. 'Do you mean Lindy knows about you and George?'

'George promised to tell her months ago, but if he so much as mentions me Lindy changes the subject,' Maggie said wryly, meeting Zoe's eyes.

Grimacing, Zoe said, 'She guesses but wants to stop him telling her, you think?'

'I'm sure! She's so used to being the most important thing in her father's life that she can't stand the idea of his marrying again. George makes me so angry—first he said we'd wait until she left school and now he wants to wait until she's at university and has settled down and made friends.' Maggie ran her hands through her hair as if wanting to tear it out by the roots. 'I have a sinking feeling Lindy isn't going to go to university. I think she'll stay here, just to keep an eye on George, she's already talking about not wanting to go to college.'

Was that because of her father, though, or because of Rory Ormond? thought Zoe as she walked down the lane to climb over a stile into Oliver's land. She was slightly drunk now; it was intensely hot and she was physically tired after her walk earlier and the strenuous riding she had done at the stables. She kept yawning and was meandering slightly on her way when a horn blazed behind her, sending her jumping into a ditch.

The car swept past and Zoe shouted after it. 'Roadhog!' She sat up and picked crushed leaves off her shirt.

Another car went by and then it stopped and backed up the lane towards her. She vaguely eyed the driver who was leaning out to stare at her.

'Hitching, darling? I'm going down south, any good to you?' the man queried after he had assessed her from head to foot and apparently decided he liked what he saw.

Zoe considered him owlishly and he got out of his car and came over to her.

'You okay?' It was quite a kindly question. He pulled her to her feet, put an arm round her, and began to steer her towards his car. That was when another car roared up and screeched to a halt. The driver leapt out and strode over to them. Zoe blinked at him, her limp body encircled by the other man's arm, and Rory said tersely, 'I'll take her now.'

'Clear off, friend. I got here first,' said the other driver. he was a short, bulky man with an obstinate face and he glowered at Rory as he tried to shoulder him out of the way.

'I know her,' said Rory, immovable in their path. 'I'll take her home, she's obviously ill.'

'Drunk,' said the driver. 'And she's hitching down south, so don't feed me any fairy tales about knowing her.'

Rory snarled something Zoe didn't catch, and the next minute the man holding her up was stretched out on the grass verge and she was being carried over Rory's shoulder in a fireman's lift and hurled into his car. Her head was whirling by then, the world was spinning in disorientating circles, and she shut her eyes and waited for it to stop revolving before she opened them again.

'You're lucky I came along, you stupid little fool,' Rory grated somewhere near by, and Zoe warily peeled her eyes open to find out if the world was standing still again.

It wasn't; it was rushing past at a worrying speed and Rory was driving with a set, brooding expression. Zoe's stomach clenched as she saw that black scowl, but she lifted her chin defiantly.

'Where did you spring from?'

'Don't you remember?' He turned his glacial eyes on her, and ran them over her in a withering distaste which made her go red. 'If I hadn't driven past back there you would have found yourself in a very nasty situation. That guy wasn't giving you a lift out of the kindness of his heart. He saw you were drunk and he meant to have you.'

Zoe shuddered. 'I'm not drunk. I almost got run down and fell into that ditch, that's all.'

Rory's brows lifted. 'That's odd—Maggie told me she thought you were too drunk to walk home but that you'd refused to ring the Naughtons for a lift or let Maggie drive you.'

'Maggie told you? You've been at the stables?'

'Maggie rang me.'

Her mouth opened in a little gasp. 'Why would she do that?' Her face was burning. What had she said to Maggie to make her think she would want Rory to come for her? She couldn't even remember; maybe she *was* drunk. Had she told Maggie too much?

'Maggie sounded more than a little light-headed herself,' Rory said drily. 'What had you two been up to?'

'I'd been riding and it was so hot and I was thirsty and Maggie had made some lemonade . . .'

'Lemonade?' he interrupted disbelievingly. 'It has quite a kick, then!'

With dignity, Zoe informed him, 'Maggie had added a touch of white wine to improve the taste.'

'A touch?'

'Or two,' Zoe conceded. She turned her head very carefully, in case the world started going round again, and stared at his grim profile. 'Did you know about Maggie and George?'

'I've got eyes in my head,' he admitted, his mouth wry.

'So have the Naughtons, but they had seen something quite different,' Zoe muttered in a confused way. 'The whole village is on the wrong track, come to that, or so Mrs Naughton said. Aren't they in for a big surprise!'

'What are you talking about?' he enquired, shooting her a glance which held derision. 'You'd better sleep it off before you go back to the farm or the Naughtons will be shocked.'

'I like Maggie,' Zoe told him, closing her eyes and yawning.

'She seems to like you,' Rory murmured from a long way off and she said, 'Good,' through another yawn, her body falling sideways until it rested on something firm and warm and comforting. Zoe cuddled down against it and fell asleep.

She woke up with a start as Rory was lifting her out of the car again. Eyes flying open, Zoe saw at once that they were in his garage and made an angry protest. 'No, take me to the farm, put me down!' She might have been rather more convincing if she hadn't winced and put a hand to her head at the same time. She had the worst headache she had ever had in her life.

'Keep still and be quiet,' Rory merely told her, carrying her into his house. He put her down quite soon, though Zoe was not much reassured to find herself lying on a bed. She immediately tried to get off again and Rory held her shoulders down, leaning over her in a disconcerting way to speak to her.

'Go back to sleep.'

He was gone before she had pulled herself together. She stumbled off the bed and followed him to the door, but the handle turned uselessly. Rory had locked her in.

Zoe banged on the door with one fist. 'Rory! Rory! Open this door!'

No reply. The house might have been empty. She couldn't hear a sound, even though she listened intently. At last she went back to the bed and sat on it, yawning, her eyes heavy and her head throbbing violently. She felt quite ill. The lemonade hadn't been that heavily spiked with wine—it must be a combination of heat, drink and exercise, she told herself. The bed looked so inviting. She curled up, determined to keep her eyes open, her head sinking into the pillows and her body slack. What on earth could she have said to Maggie to make her jump to the conclusion that she would want Rory to come for her? She wished she could remember what she had told Maggie; she hated to think that she had admitted ... what? What was there to admit? she asked herself angrily—but she was too tired now to think, so she just let go and drifted off into a warm oblivion.

When she woke up it was dark in the room and for a second she was totally disorientated and couldn't remember where she was, then her nose twitched, picking up a delicious smell.

Coffee! she thought, sitting up. Her eyes flew round the room without recognising anything, although she had now remembered what had happened and how she had got here. When her stare reached the door she was shaken to find it standing open. Rory had been in here while she slept! She got off the bed and quietly tiptoed to the door, wondering if she would be able to get out of the house before Rory realised she was awake, but no sooner had she crept into the corridor than she found herself face to face with Rory.

'Hallo, Sleeping Beauty,' he mocked. 'I was just bringing you some coffee. How's the head?'

Zoe backed instinctively, running a hand over her dishevelled hair. 'Okay, thank you.' She must have slept for hours and her head no longer ached, but she winced as Rory callously turned on the light. It was far too bright; her eyes squinted bitterly at him. 'I'd better get back to the farm before the Naughtons start ringing the police!'

'I've rung them,' Rory informed her with bland indifference to her look of dismay.

'What did you say to them?'

'I told them you were with me and wouldn't be back for a while.' He put the tray of coffee down on the bedside table. 'Drink this, and then why don't you have a shower to wake yourself up?'

'I can have a bath at the farm,' she protested.

'I've made supper—it'll be ready in half an hour,' Rory told her, walking away.

She pursued him. 'Look, I'd much rather . . .'

'Drink your coffee.'

The door shut and she stared at it, her hands curling into fists and her teeth tight. He was a maddening man!

Who did he think he was, giving her orders, running her life for her? She backed and sat gingerly on the edge of the bed to drink some of the strong coffee he had brought. It helped; she had to admit that. Her eyes roved around the bedroom—his? she speculated, curiously inspecting the cool, quiet colours. He had chosen a soft blue-grey for the walls and the curtains were almost primrose, a buttery colour reflected in the cover on the quilt and the fine cotton sheets. The landscapes hanging on the walls were his; delicate watercolours of the sky and sea, of the fields and cliffs. Zoe wandered around, admiring them. He had grown as an artist since they last met. She had been too young to recognise quite how much talent he had; she could see that now.

Of course, she knew far more about art today. In the advertising business, art played a very important role, and Zoe worked with some of the best commercial artists in the world. She had soon realised she ought to know what they were talking about when they discussed the graphics which would best suit the product. She had read books, visited galleries and even gone to evening art classes one year. She had no talent herself, but it had taught her to recognise and admire talent in others and she knew very well why George Ash called Rory a genius. He was brilliant, there was no disputing that.

She slowly walked into the bathroom and bolted the door before taking a leisurely shower that fully woke her up.

Towelling vigorously afterwards, she wryly recognised that during the seven years since she and Rory met she had unconsciously been deeply interested in art because of him. She had never admitted it to herself until now; convincing herself that her fascination was entirely due to a desire to improve her understanding of the advertising world. It was easy to fool oneself. She had needed to think up a good reason for doing what she couldn't help doing anyway.

She put on her jeans and borrowed one of Rory's cotton T-shirts, because her own shirt was grass-stained, then went in search of him.

He was in the kitchen, laying a varnished pine table, setting out pretty Spanish cork-backed mats and cutlery and wine glasses. There was one white rose in a slim green vase in the centre of the table; looking at it, Zoe suddenly remembered the rose he had put in her hair at George Ash's party, and her face burned.

Had he chosen one white rose deliberately—or was it a pure coincidence? Her eyes flashed. She didn't believe that—there was nothing either pure or a coincidence about it! Rory had her here alone and he intended to make a pass.

'Feel better?' he asked without looking round, his lean body straightening as he finished working on the table. He surveyed what he had done, then turned to look at her, narrowing his eyes as he took in her expression.

'Still in a temper?' He walked over to the oven and picked up some oven gloves. 'Maybe you're hungry. Sit down, I'm just going to serve our supper.'

Zoe sat down wordlessly and watched him coming back with a large casserole dish from which a delicious smell rose.

'You like chicken, don't you?' he said casually, and she nodded, wondering if that was a guess or if he remembered an evening she remembered vividly. They had eaten at a tiny auberge in a village in Provence; coq au vin with an incredible bouqet to the casserole, wine-rich liquid and button mushrooms and tiny onions. They had eaten it on the auberge terrace just above a vineyard; dusk had fallen and they had sat and talked for hours, drinking coffee in incredibly small cups, their eyes on each other, their hands sometimes touching. All the other guests had gone; the *patron* hadn't disturbed them, though. He had gone about his evening routine; clearing tables, washing up, locking up. They had been aware of him in the background, but nothing had mattered. It had been a dream they walked in with open eyes.

'Can I help?' she asked huskily, and Rory shook his head.

'I can manage—I'm very domesticated.' His grey eyes mocked her, then he deftly served the food on to warm plates. He had made a coq au vin, she saw, as the pieces of chicken, the mushrooms and onions and round, small potatoes were placed on her plate. Her eyes skimmed his face and Rory grinned at her.

'Remember the Auberge St Jacques?'

Her high colour was answer enough, she looked away, hating him. How could he mention that evening? It had been one of the moments of pure happiness she had felt that summer; a special moment in her life. What had it meant to him? Had it meant anything?

He sat down opposite and leaned over to fill her glass with a clear, golden wine. Zoe saw the label on the bottle and the hair prickled on the nape of her neck. He had served the same wine, too. She had known nothing about wine before she met Rory—he had enjoyed introducing her to French wines, taking her to local vineyards to taste their wines, explaining why you drank one wine with fish, another with a dessert. She had been a wide-eyed innocent and he had educated her.

Her teeth met and she kept her eyes down. What an ego trip he must have had! That, no doubt, was why he remembered it so well!

'So Maggie told you about her problem?' Rory drawled, filling his own glass. 'George is too scrupulous about Lindy's feelings. If he's not careful, he'll lose Maggie altogether, and you can't blame her for resenting having to take second place to his daughter even now the girl's of age. The trouble with Lindy is that she's trying to have her cake and eat it.'

'What does that mean?' asked Zoe coldly.

'She's acting like a telescope,' he told her with dry amusement. 'One minute she's very grown-up and doesn't want her father to tell her what to do—it's her life and she's quite capable of living it! The next minute, she's a little girl again, making poor old George feel guilty for wanting to have a life of his own, clinging to him and sulking if he sees too much of Maggie.'

Zoe ate some of the coq au vin and found it surprisingly good. 'Did you really make this?' she asked him.

'Don't sound so incredulous! Yes, I did—why shouldn't I be able to cook? The best chefs are always men.'

'I don't remember you doing much cooking,' she began, then stopped, wishing she hadn't brought up the past again.

'In Provence?' he said casually. 'No, I was too busy painting there.' His eyes flicked her way, filled with glimmering mockery. 'My mind was on other things.'

She ignored that. 'Have you talked to Lindy about her father and Maggie?'

'I've tried. She doesn't want to listen. She doesn't want

him to marry again; she thinks it's selfish, disgraceful.' He made a face. 'She's horribly young, and the young are always puritanical and arrogant.'

'I wasn't,' Zoe involuntarily denied, and his smile made her heart stop.

'It was a different form of arrogance, but it was there—you were just as horribly young, and just as blindly unaware of it, as sure you knew everything. You frightened me, you were so reckless. You flung yourself into life as if there were no tomorrow.'

Zoe's head was bent and she was automatically eating without really tasting what she put into her mouth and swallowed. She had been reckless, she couldn't deny it. She had been wildly in love and blind to the way he felt. Yes, she had been horribly young.

'You're making excuses for yourself,' she muttered when she could speak, and her voice vibrated with bitterness.

'Be honest, Zoe—would it have made it any easier if I'd explained why I was going?' Rory asked quietly.

'Yes, of course!' she said, her head lifting to stare at him, and then their eyes met and his held her stare, his gaze steady and insistent. There was a little silence, then she gave a harsh sigh.

'Perhaps not.' Would it have made it less painful if she had known? Once he had gone she had realised he didn't love her and she had broken up inside. Being told in advance wouldn't have made it easier to bear. It would have been worse, far worse, to sit there listening while Rory told her he didn't love her and was going away. She might have cried and clung to him, and the humiliation of remembering that afterwards would have made it worse. A quick, clean ending was shock, but there was no lingering uncertainty, no hope, no memory of the way she had taken the news to haunt her.

'When we first met I didn't even realise you were only seventeen,' said Rory with grim flatness. 'You fooled me completely. You looked at least twenty in that bikini.'

She remembered it as if it had been yesterday—the burning sun, the ochre and burnt umber of the hillside behind her hotel, the shimmer of the olive-trees and the darkness of the cypresses and Rory watching her as he painted the hotel for the manager. It was a commission offered on the spur of the moment and would help Rory pay for his food and rent, but Zoe hadn't known that. She had watched him with fascination as she sunbathed on a lounger in the garden. He had looked up at the nineteenth-century building, assessing the smudged blue shadows on the old white walls, the shutters on the windows to keep the rooms cool during the sun's height, then he had gone back to his canvas, his blue-black head shining in the sun as he bent forward to brush in a little yellow here, a little green there.

Zoe had been wearing the skimpiest of bikinis; gaily coloured cotton which showed off her pale tan. She wanted to be as brown as the French girls in the village. Before she met Rory she had sunbathed every afternoon, risking sunstroke in spite of the hotel proprietor's advice and warning frowns.

Rory had painted in brief white shorts and a loose black top which he shed later, leaving his deep chest bare. He had been tanned as deeply as the natives; his skin a glowing mahogany.

'You didn't act like a teenager,' said Rory, breaking into her memories. 'No blushing and giggling, like some of the English girls who had been staying at the hotel.

You were cool and quiet and deceptively mature. It didn't occur to me for a long time that you weren't even eighteen—let alone that you were still at school. You were working there alone and I assumed you'd been at work for some time. When I discovered the truth, it knocked me sideways.'

'I never lied to you—you didn't ask!'

'You must have realised what I thought!'

She had, of course. It had been tremendously flattering to a girl of seventeen to have someone as exciting and glamorous as Rory Ormond taking a very personal interest in her. She had soon realised that he thought her older than she really was, but she hadn't wanted to admit her true age, in case it changed the way he saw her. She had gloried in pretending to a sophistication she didn't possess, but Rory had gradually caught on and finally confronted her with some curt questions to which she had to give honest answers.

A week later he had vanished from the village and her life, and she had been too distraught to think very clearly about the reason for the change in him.

'Is that why?' she asked him now in a low, unsteady voice. 'Did you go like that because I was too young for you?'

'Why else?' Rory said grimly. 'I was going to be thirty on my next birthday, a fact that was weighing pretty heavily on my mind all that summer. It's quite a milestone, and I'd been realising a lot of other things, too. My private life was very empty when I was in France. I hadn't met anyone who mattered to me for years and I was restless and bored. I suppose I was ready to fall for the next attractive girl I met, and it happened to be you, but then I found out that you were just a kid, a schoolgirl little more than half my age. And do you know who told me? The old guy who ran that hotel you worked at! He'd seen us together and he was shocked, he said. You were in his care and he had failed your parents. An innocent schoolgirl had been seduced under his roof. He was scathing about my morals and told me never to set foot in his hotel again, he made me feel about two feet high, but I simply didn't believe it. I tore off to find you and ask you, and you admitted it. I spent a few very bad days and nights trying to think what to do, but I really had no option.'

Seven years ago, Zoe would have argued with him, pleaded, insisted that she was quite old enough for him, said she would leave school, clung to him, telling him she loved him, and cried her eyes out.

What would Rory have done then? She felt a strange, painful relief that he hadn't allowed her to make that scene or let her imagine that they had a future, because she could see now that it would never have worked. She had been too young, she had a lot of growing up to do and she would have found marriage to someone like Rory far too difficult. He was too far ahead of her in every possible sense. If he had been crazy enough to risk it, disaster would probably have lain ahead sooner or later. They had met too soon, she had been too deeply in love, and that emotion had been beyond her control or understanding, it had grown too fast, and like some greenhouse plant it had been too fragile and too easy to kill.

'You do see that?' he said quietly. 'I'm sorry if you were hurt at the time, Zoe, but I did what I thought was best for you. It was over, and the sooner I went the better.'

Childishly, she resented the finality of his tone. He couldn't have had any real feelings about her if he could walk away so calmly without looking back.

'You could have left a letter,' she muttered.

'I thought of that, but it seemed best just to go! I knew you would be hurt, whatever I did, but I hoped you'd get over it sooner if it was sudden and final.'

'Final,' she murmured, frowning. 'Yes, it was that.' There was no point in telling him how that cruel ending had blighted her life ever since, how reluctant she had been to feel anything for anyone in case it happened again. She had been too young to feel the icy touch of frost.

'Finish your chicken,' he said, watching her through his black lashes.

'I've had enough, thank you,' she said, pushing her plate away. 'I'm very tired. Would you drive me back to the farm?'

'Now?' Rory said harshly.

'Yes, please.'

'No comment on what I told you?'

Zoe looked coolly at him. 'What is there to say? I can see why you went, it's very understandable. I was too young and you were wise enough to realise it. What else is there to say?'

He got to his feet, his face hard. 'Nothing, I suppose.'

'Don't turn moody,' she said lightly. Why was he glowering at her? What had he expected? Had he wanted absolution, to be told that he hadn't hurt her beyond bearing, that really it had all been wonderful fun, a teenage dream, and what was a broken heart between friends? If he had hoped for that, she wasn't giving in to him. Rory had destroyed years of her life and made it impossible for her to risk caring for any other man—she wasn't going to lie about it, merely to ease his conscience!

'Moody?' he repeated in a voice that made the hair lift on her head. 'What are you talking about?'

Zoe decided the sooner he dropped her at the farm the better. She would lose her own temper any minute. She wasn't having him glare at her like that or snap like an angry crocodile just because she tried to keep this on a civilised plane.

She made it to the door and glanced back. 'Can we go?'

Rory's expression made her nerves jump violently, but he followed her, through the house and into the garage through a side door. She went ahead, and winced as he stamped after her. Surely he didn't have to slam *every* door? It was typical of the man, though, that he should become impossible simply because she wouldn't soothe his uneasiness over having walked out on her without a word seven years ago. If he ran her down in his car, he would no doubt expect her to lift her dying head and moan, 'It was all my own fault!'

He drove through the dangerous moonlight without speaking or looking at her, and whenever she glanced his way she was shaken by the lethal ice of his expression. In this mood, Rory could sink the *Titanic*, and Zoe had never felt less like taking him on. She hoped she would be able to slide away into the farmhouse without having to say anything but goodnight. He pulled up with such a jerk that she almost went through the windscreen; her seat-belt saved her and she bit down on her inner lip to stop herself turning to shout at Rory. Instead she reached for the door.

'Wait a minute,' he said, and her heart sank. She gave him a wary glance over her shoulder and felt her stomach clench at the violence in his face.

'I just remembered,' he said through his teeth. 'Why

did you come here with Oliver? If it wasn't to see me?'

Her eyes widened and dilated and her colour came and went in waves, and Rory watched her with narrowed eyes and a slow, curling smile.

'Well?' he asked in a husky, intimate murmur, his smile deepening the little lines around his mouth.

Panic made her lie. 'I've always fancied the idea of being a farmer's wife,' she said, and he stopped smiling and stared at her in disbelief. 'Oliver's gorgeous, too,' she added recklessly. 'Such marvellous fair hair and skin— and he'll be a perfect husband. It's lucky I get on so well with his family.'

It didn't matter whether he believed her or not. The sheer surprise of it had apparently paralysed him, and while he was getting his breath back Zoe got out of the car and fled.

If she hadn't lied, Rory might have touched her, kissed her, the way he had in the garden at the Ash house, and Zoe couldn't have borne that. She was going away again tomorrow morning and she didn't intend to see Rory again. It was over, really over this time. No frozen pain, no bitter wariness about other men, no reluctance to get involved—from now on she was going to meet life in a very different way, and one day maybe she would fall in love again and this time there might be a happy ending for her. The prospect shimmered like a rainbow after a dark storm, and she was not going to let Rory ruin it for her.

He might have gone away seven years ago because she was too young, but however old she had been there wouldn't have been a future for her with Rory Ormond, because he wasn't the marrying kind. He wouldn't give her the sort of love she wanted. He was too self-absorbed.

He still found her attractive, Zoe knew that. She had known from the minute they met again and Rory had looked at her, his eyes dark and glowing with desire. He wanted her and he would take her if he could; but sooner or later he would vanish again, with or without a word of explanation, because he was a rover, in every sense of the word. He travelled a great deal, painting wherever he happened to be, and he always travelled light. He didn't take anyone with him. A fellow-traveller would slow him up, cramp his style.

Zoe wasn't prepared to have another brief affair with him, and she felt a bitter sense of triumph and elation as she tried to get to sleep that night. This time she was turning the tables. This time she was vanishing without a word. She hoped Rory would appreciate the irony.

CHAPTER SEVEN

OLIVER was surprisingly cheerful on the drive down to London, and whistled through his teeth in a piercing way that made Zoe wince. She hadn't slept much the night before, and was feeling distinctly under the weather this morning, for which she blamed her sleepless night, not the fact that she was saying goodbye to Rory Ormond a second time. She had no intention of ever regretting that. She was going to be very cool about the whole thing, but she wished Oliver weren't quite so bright-eyed and glowing with health, because for some inexplicable reason that made her gloomy and resentful. In keeping with her own funereal mood, Oliver should have been silent and grim.

Catching his eye, she was even more annoyed when he winked, and she asked coldly, 'Something funny?'

'Last night . . .' Oliver began, then had to swerve dangerously as a lorry thundered past and slotted in before him. He slammed a hand on his horn and at the same time put a foot on his brake, so absorbed that he didn't see the hot colour sweep up Zoe's face or the look of dismay in her eyes.

'Damn stupid fool!' he yelled, while she eyed him sideways and wondered urgently what on earth he had been going to say.

But his good humour came back a moment later and he calmed down enough for her to prompt him, 'What were you going to say just now?'

He looked blank, then laughed. 'Oh, yes—Lindy and George came round last night to deliver some books for the church jumble sale, and while they were there Ormond rang up to tell us you were at his place and not to wait up for you because you wouldn't be back until quite late.'

Zoe's face was pink. 'I wasn't all that late, actually—it was only half past ten!' She paused, then added hurriedly, 'We had dinner.'

Oliver shrugged that aside, he wasn't really interested in what she and Rory had been doing, he was bursting with other news.

'Anyway, Mum told us all, and then said she was surprised at you, you knew about Rory and Maggie and she hadn't thought you were the type to steal another woman's man.'

Tight-lipped, Zoe said, 'I wasn't doing anything of the kind!' She paused, frowning, as it occurred to her that if George Ash had no idea of the gossip about Maggie and Rory it must have come as quite a shock to him when Mrs Naughton started talking like that! 'What did George say?' she asked hesitantly, wondering if she ought to mention what Maggie had told her. How could she? Maggie had been talking in strict confidence and obviously didn't want anyone to know until George got up the courage to tell his daughter.

Oliver looked bewildered. 'George? He didn't say anything. Lindy did, though—she really lost her temper and she called you . . .' He went a little red and mumbled, 'Well, names.'

Zoe couldn't help laughing, but sobered again a second

later because it really wasn't funny, was it? Poor Lindy. Not long ago she must have believed that the whole world revolved around her, then her father had begun taking more interest in Maggie Thorn, and Lindy's cosy little world began to crumble. Whether what Lindy felt for Rory was real or not; whether he was a father figure or something more adult, Lindy must be getting hurt, and Zoe felt sorry for her. She had been there; she knew what the girl must be feeling.

Oliver hadn't finished, though. Complacently he added, 'And then she said some vicious things about Ormond. I expected George to stop her, but he didn't, he just sat there and didn't say a word.'

Zoe frowned. George must have been shattered, but the shock might do some good. It might make him take a decision at last, force him to realise that he couldn't ask Maggie to wait indefinitely. Men could be so blind and self-obsessed—George had probably been very complacent about Maggie, he hadn't expected anyone else to show an interest in her. Not very flattering for Maggie, no wonder she had been so angry with him lately! It wasn't simply that George was putting his daughter before Maggie. He was blithely over-confident; sure that she would wait for him until the crack of doom, no doubt.

'I told Lindy I was driving you back to London today,' Oliver said with a broad smile. 'And she said she'd come with me to the dance on Saturday, so my idea of having you at the farm paid off, didn't it? I don't think Lindy will look at Ormond again. He's finished as far as she's concerned, she despises him—she told me so.'

Zoe looked incredulously at him. Did he really believe that? He didn't know a thing about women or the way their minds worked. No doubt Lindy was jealous and angry and vengeful at the moment, but she wouldn't stay that way long. Oliver was a darling and Zoe had become very fond of him, but he wasn't in Rory Ormond's class, and Lindy was not going to give up on Rory without a fight.

'Well, good luck,' she told him drily.

He took it literally, of course. 'Thanks,' he said, bright-eyed and floating on a pink cloud. 'I really appreciate everything you did—luring Ormond away, I mean. I know it wasn't much fun for you.'

'No,' said Zoe. 'I wouldn't describe it as fun.'

'I know he's a . . .' Oliver bit back one word and hunted for something that would convey exactly how he saw Rory Ormond. 'King-sized rat,' he decided was the very description.

'Yes, he's that,' she agreed. All farmers hated rats, she knew that. They were the biggest headache in the farmyard; fouling grain, killing baby chickens, eating everything. She knew why Oliver called Rory a rat; there was no stronger word to him.

'I was sure you could handle him, though,' said Oliver with blithe confidence.

'Thank you,' Zoe said, wishing she had. The only handling of Rory Ormond she would ever do in future would be from a very great distance—the other end of the universe, for instance—and with great care and protective clothing.

Oliver carried her case into her flat, stayed ten minutes for a cup of tea and then left. He was, she gathered, eager to get home again in case Rory Ormond had treacherously undermined him with Lindy. Oliver hoped to keep them apart for ever after this, and Zoe felt very sorry for him as she shut her front door on him. He wouldn't have a chance of success with Lindy until Rory had gone out of her life for good. Zoe was sure that that would happen one day; the only question was—when? Rory never stayed anywhere for long. He might like Cumbria, but he would be off one day on his travels and he wouldn't be taking Lindy with him. He always travelled alone.

Perhaps it was because he was an artist and didn't want anything personal interfering with his work? Rory had charm and personality, but even when he smiled and talked amusingly there was a still, quiet, secret place at the centre of his nature which Zoe had always sensed, and which she guessed was an intrinsic part of his art. Rory liked his own company, he needed to be alone for large stretches of time. He often didn't want to talk; his whole mind was occupied and there was no energy to spare for anyone or anything else.

In one way she hadn't been totally surprised when he left without saying a word. It made sense that if he was going he would not say anything to her. Rory didn't talk about the things that mattered most to him, he kept one side of himself hidden from her.

If she hadn't been crazy enough to believe he loved her she wouldn't have been so shocked by the abrupt ending. *That* was in character, and she was sure he would leave Cumbria in exactly the same way, as suddenly and silently.

Fiona came home just after six-thirty and stopped in surprise as she walked into the kitchen and saw Zoe. 'Oh, you're back!'

'Typical Civil Service comment—always state the

obvious as loudly as possible!' Zoe was tossing a green salad, and Fiona leaned over and snatched a sliver of green pepper which she popped into her mouth and crunched with enjoyment.

'You've come back very touchy. I did warn you,' she said, eyeing Zoe sideways with a sympathetic grimace.

'Don't say I told you so, please! That would be too much.' Zoe walked over to the table with the bowl of salad while Fiona was taking off her fitted grey jacket.

'It's so damn hot!' she complained, as Zoe turned to survey her ruefully. Fiona always looked fabulous, but today she was austerely elegant—the charcoal-grey jacket and pleated skirt, the lavender silk shirt and loosely knotted purple tie had a touch of French chic, and with her smooth blonde hair and luminous eyes the combination was unbeatable. She must have stopped the traffic in that, Zoe thought, feeling scruffy in her old cotton summer dress. She had put it on because it was light and cool, but it had been washed until it had almost no colour, and it didn't have much shape either.

'Going out tonight?' she asked, and Fiona shook her head.

'I've brought some paperwork home instead.'

'What happened to the stockbroker?'

'He was a bore.'

'I always thought so.'

'I know. You made that crystal clear, and it was none of your damn business.'

Zoe curtsied, a finger under her chin. 'Sorry. I won't talk about him if you don't talk about my private life.'

Fiona took off her purple tie and deftly made a noose of it. 'You're cunningly trying to stop me asking questions about what went on in Yorkshire!' she said, advancing with the noose towards Zoe.

'Cumbria!' protested Zoe, laughing.

'Well, Cumbria, then—does it matter? Same sort of scenery and same sheep.'

'Nothing of the kind, it's quite different landscape around where Oliver lives. Do you want supper? I've got a quiche, and some strawberries for dessert. I thought I'd treat myself.'

'Sounds lovely.' Fiona swung the purple tie from her wrist, her face serious. 'Are you all right, Zoe? You didn't get your heart broken all over again, did you?'

Zoe put a hand to her chest, grimacing. 'No, my heart's all in one piece and going tickety-tick as normal.' But she didn't quite meet Fiona's eyes, and her friend shrewdly noticed as much and frowned.

'Now why don't I believe you?'

'Because you've got a suspicious mind,' Zoe told her, becoming very busy again as she finished laying the table. 'If you're going to wash before we eat hadn't you better get moving?'

'I always know when you're hiding something,' Fiona informed her drily. 'You change the subject in a very obvious way.'

'Well, I'm certainly sorry if I'm obvious, but I'm also hungry and I want to eat, so if you're joining me can you make up your mind soon?' Zoe opened a bottle of sparkling mineral water, and Fiona's brows rose.

'There's white wine in the fridge!'

Zoe shuddered. 'No, thanks! I'll stick to Perrier.' The very mention of the word wine reminded her of Maggie and her spiked lemonade. If she hadn't let Maggie refill her glass so many times she wouldn't have wandered along the road in a sleepy daze and fallen into that ditch, nor would she have let Rory put her into his car and take her home with him. If she ever saw Maggie Thorn again she would tell her *never* to put wine in her lemonade! There was something so innocuous and deceptive about an iced jug of lemonade that fooled you into thinking another glass wouldn't hurt you. The taste of the lemon hid the wine, just as Rory Ormond's smiling eyes hid his potential danger.

'Hangover?' Fiona enquired shrewdly, and Zoe shrugged.

'One white wine too many! And I'll have to get back to work tomorrow, so I'll need all my wits about me!'

When she got into the office the following morning she found it practically deserted because everyone was in a campaign meeting in the boardroom. One girl was at the reception desk, operating the small switchboard and typing at the same time. She grinned at Zoe and told her where the rest of the staff were, adding that they should be out of conference any minute, so Zoe went into Joe Holt's office to wait for him. It was twenty minutes before he appeared, and by then she had read her way through a pile of old copies of *Punch* and was failing to find anything funny. She seemed to have mislaid her sense of humour in Cumbria.

'Where did you spring from?' queried Joe in smiling surprise. A large, broad man with sleek black hair and a massive head, he was in his early forties and combined an amazing presence with charm and wit. Joe could be very funny, could coax a smile out of the toughest businessman, but he could also turn on power that froze the blood in your veins. 'I've been ringing you for days and that flatmate of yours kept telling me you were away, in a very mysterious tone, as if you'd run off with the milkman to live it up in Bournemouth.'

'It was Cumbria, actually, and I'd run off with a sheep-farmer,' Zoe said lightly.

He waited, smiling encouragement. It was one of his techniques for getting information out of people. Faced with his warm, friendly silence, they found themselves confiding things torture wouldn't have dragged out of them.

'Boring animals, sheep,' Zoe went on. 'And prone to some horrific diseases.' She side-tracked into a description of a few the Naughtons had told her about, and Joe's smile congealed on his face.

'I can see why you came back to London and deserted the sheep-farmer,' he interrupted at last. 'Is that what he talked about all the time?'

'He was dedicated to his work!' she said blandly, and he began to laugh. 'Talking of work,' she added, 'Fiona said that when you rang you mentioned a campaign you want me to work on.'

'That's right,' said Joe, sitting down behind his desk and at once becoming businesslike. 'Jamieson's are going to be launching a whole new range of skin-care products in the autumn next year and they want a major launch, with publicity beginning well in front.'

'Jamiesons . . .' she sighed, and met his wry eyes.

'I know, I know. He fancies you and that's a slight problem, but Rudy Jamieson isn't hard to manage, is he? He doesn't turn nasty or get difficult, he just keeps on trying. Have lunch, be nice to him—keep him at a distance. What harm is there in that?'

'It's tiring, that's all,' Zoe retorted. 'You don't have to put up with the pressure. I wouldn't mind, but he fancies himself as much as he fancies me. I never met a more conceited man! That's why he won't take no for an answer. He simply doesn't believe I can resist him. He can't.'

Joe grinned.'You've got a wicked tongue on you, Zoe Stroud.' He picked up a pencil and tapped it on his desk thoughtfully, eyeing her. 'He asked for you,' he pointed out.

'Who's surprised? It isn't my creative flair he's interested in, though! Professionally, Rudy's admiration isn't much of a compliment.'

'It's a very lucrative contract,' he told her gently, and she lifted her shoulders in a defeated shrug.

'Okay, I give in—let me have all the paperwork and I'll start thinking.'

Pleased with her, Joe smiled benevolently. 'Tell you what—I'll fix the lunch with Rudy and I'll come too. He can't give you any hassle while I'm there, can he?'

Zoe thanked him cordially, but when she saw Fiona that night she prophesied gloomily that even the presence of another man wouldn't deter Rudy Jamieson's sexual pursuit.

'He takes every opportunity he can! Always touching your hand, smiling meaningfully, murmuring sweet nothings, managing to put an arm round you. The man's a pest!'

'What's the Rudy short for? Rudolph?'

'Rudyard—as in Kipling!'

'How old is he, for heaven's sake?'

'Late thirties, I suppose.'

'Married?'

'I wish he was! No, he probably thinks it would be a tragedy for the opposite sex if he limited himself to one woman. You must have seen his picture in the gossip columns. Rudy has women the way a dog has fleas.'

'But he still fancies you?'

'Not very flattering, is it? Being one among so many?'

'Is he handsome?' asked Fiona with interest, eyes bright.

'He thinks so.'

'Zoe, I really want to know—is he good-looking?'

'Unfortunately I hate to say yes.'

'Sexy?'

'I can't give you an unbiased answer because I don't find him in the least bit sexy, but from the way he scores with other women I may be in the minority.'

Fiona sat on the floor in a pair of silk lounging-pyjamas, her body in a semi-lotus position, her feet curled up on her knees. She smiled to herself in a way that made Zoe's eyebrows rise. She knew that smile. She had seen it on Rudy Jamieson often enough, and now that she came to think of it they were two of a kind—as silkily predatory as alley-cats and as fond of luxury and the good life.

'Where did you say you and Joe were having lunch with him?' Fiona asked.

'What are you plotting now?' queried Zoe, but told her the name of the restaurant.

'I think . . .' Fiona began, and stopped as the doorbell rang. They both looked at the clock, frowning. It was gone nine o'clock.

'Who can that be at his hour?' pondered Fiona without moving from her meditating stance.

'There's only one way to find out!' Zoe reluctantly pulled herself out of her armchair; and went to open the door, expecting to find one of Fiona's men outside. Her jaw dropped when she found Maggie standing there, her face pale and uncertain, a suitcase in her hand.

'Maggie? What are you doing here?'

Maggie's pallor deepened. 'I'm sorry, I know it's very late, but I've been trying to find a hotel room and I couldn't get in anywhere and I wondered . . . I'm sorry, I should never have come on impulse like this without booking a room first, but I hadn't realised how full up London hotels would be, but . . . look, I shouldn't have bothered you, don't worry, I'll find something.' She turned to go, her suitcase banging against the wall, and Zoe leapt after her and caught her arm, pulling her back to the flat.

'Stop gibbering and come in—of course you can stay, as long as you don't mind sleeping on a couch. It's quite a big couch and it is quite comfortable. We often have people sleeping on it and they don't complain.'

She pushed Maggie into the sitting-room, took her case and put it down, while Maggie and Fiona were staring at each other in dumb surmise.

'Fiona, this is Maggie Thorn. I met her in Cumbria. Maggie, this is my flatmate, Fiona.'

Maggie said miserably, 'Hallo. I'm sorry to disturb you at this time of night.'

Fiona uncoiled herself with smooth economy of movement and stood up. Giving Maggie a smile, she offered, 'Why don't I make us all some hot chocolate?

Are you hungry, Maggie? We have some cold meat and salad, or there are lots of eggs.'

Maggie shuddered. 'No, I'm not at all hungry, thanks,' Zoe got the impression Maggie never meant to eat again, and Fiona's quick darted glance showed that she had picked up the same message. Discreetly sliding out of the room, Fiona left them alone, and Zoe patted the couch.

'Try it for comfort.'

Maggie sat down on the edge of it and began another muddled apology. 'I'm sorry, if I'd realised you didn't live here alone . . . I didn't mean to make a nuisance of myself . . . I . . .'

'What's happened?' Zoe cut her short. 'What made you run away? And who's looking after the horses?'

A faint gleam of the capable Maggie she had met in Cumbria came back then. 'I asked one of my pupils to stay in the house and keep an eye on things. She's keen to work in a stable and often helps me at weekends, so she knows what to do. The horses will be okay.'

'Good,' said Zoe, pleased to have got a calmer answer out of her. 'Now, what's the problem? George?' Who else could it be? Maggie looked like a three-day corpse, and only a man could make a sensible woman look like that.

Nodding, Maggie muttered, 'He . . . he . . .'

'He'd heard the village gossip about you and Rory?' guessed Zoe, seeing that she wasn't going to get anywhere with Maggie unless she prompted her.

A wild look shot across Maggie's face. 'You didn't tell him?'

'No, it was Mrs Naughton. I heard about it from Oliver. So what did George have to say about it? Didn't you explain that it was all moonshine?'

'He didn't give me a chance. He was very angry—he thought I'd been seeing Rory to punish him, that I wanted to force his hand and make him tell Lindy about us. I couldn't get a word out. George shouted, and I've never heard George shout like that before! He's such a quiet man.'

'Jealousy does funny things to people,' said Zoe, her mouth wry. It had done some very strange things to her—jealousy was like acid burning away inside you, warping and deforming.

'Then he suddenly stormed out,' Maggie went on in a shaky voice. 'He said it was over! He said he could see he'd been wrong about me, I wasn't the sort of woman he'd thought I was—if I'd really cared about him I wouldn't have tried to hurt him just to get my own way, and if I preferred Rory I could have him.'

'What a fathead!' Zoe said impatiently. 'I thought George had more sense.'

'I suddenly couldn't bear it,' Maggie half-sobbed. 'I had to get away, so I just threw some things in a case and got in my car and started driving. I didn't really think where I was going. I sort of woke up on the motorway to London, and then I realised I hadn't made any arrangements about the horses so I found a phone-box and rang Nella and asked her if she'd take charge until I got back. I don't know why I came to London, except that I knew you lived here and I'd talked to you about George and you were the only one I felt I could talk to now.'

Zoe was touched. 'I'm glad you did come,' she assured Maggie. 'I'm sure George will calm down and realise how wrong he was! By the time you get back he'll have talked to Rory and found out that there was nothing to the rumours. Rory will soon make him see sense.'

Maggie sniffed and blew her nose into a crisp new handkerchief. 'If he talks to Rory! Knowing George he won't want to talk about it.'

'Ring Rory and ask him to tackle George, then!'

'I couldn't!' protested Maggie, horrified, and nothing Zoe could say would make her change her mind.

Fiona came back with their hot chocolate in the middle of that argument and Zoe left her to talk to Maggie, excusing herself by saying she was going to find some extra pillows and a quilt for Maggie to use on the couch that night.

There was a telephone on the bedside table in Fiona's room; she loved talking on the phone in bed at night and didn't scruple to ring her latest boy-friend at an unearthly hour merely to murmur flirtatiously to him for as long as it took her to feel sleepy.

Zoe had to ask the telephone exchange to look up Rory's telephone number, but eventually she was given it and dialled. At first she thought he wasn't at home, then the ringing stopped and she heard his voice; deep and abrupt and very far away.

'This is Zoe,' she said, and there was a silence. She heard him breathing and said quickly, 'Rory? Are you there?'

'Yes,' he said huskily. 'Where are you?'

'London. Look, Maggie's here—she's in quite a state. Apparently George had a row with her over you and she was so upset she bolted down to London. Can you talk to George and make him see the whole thing is nonsense? Maggie's very unhappy.'

There was another long silence, then he laughed oddly. 'Funnily enough, George is here now. He's in quite a state, too. Apparently Maggie has disappeared, and George has rung the police because he's worried about her.'

'Oh, no,' she said, aghast.

'I'm afraid so. Maggie is officially a missing person at the moment.'

'But she rang one of her pupils to explain where she was—isn't the girl at the stable?'

'That's what alerted George. He went round there and found this girl in charge, and she told him Maggie had sounded very strange on the phone. The girl's obviously the melodramatic sort. She hinted at suicide.'

'Suicide? Maggie?' Zoe's voice rose. 'How very stupid. Doesn't George know Maggie better than that? Running up here to see me is as crazy as Maggie gets.'

'Well, you said it, not me,' drawled Rory, and she grimaced angrily.

'Anyway, will you please tell George that there has never been anything between you and Maggie and I'll get Maggie to go back home as soon as I can.' She stopped speaking, listening to his breathing and feeling a strange, unbearable intimacy with him. 'Goodnight,' she said, her voice almost a whisper.

'Zoe!' Rory said sharply, and she gripped the phone so tightly that her knuckles turned white.

'Yes?'

'Goodnight,' was all he said, though, and Zoe put the phone down. He hadn't expressed any reaction to her sudden departure for London. He obviously didn't care whether she went or stayed. She stared down at the phone, her eyes burning. Her emotions were in such a stupid muddle; she was tugged first one way then another, and she couldn't think straight when her mind was always in confusion. It had hurt to hear his voice. It would always hurt.

She turned and walked out of the room, stopped at the airing-cupboard to collect spare pillows and a quilt, and went back to Maggie and Fiona, who were talking pleasantly about horses. Zoe was surprised to hear Fiona talking so knowledgeably about them; she hadn't realised Fiona rode. When she said so Fiona laughed.

'I don't now. I did at one time.' She yawned. 'Well, I'm tired and I have to get up early so I'll say goodnight. Sleep well, Maggie.'

Zoe didn't stay up much later. She decided Maggie needed a good night's sleep, so she helped her make up a bed on the couch and then said goodnight too. She was so tired that she fell asleep almost at once and woke up to hear the doorbell ringing.

She yawned and stumbled out of bed, hearing Fiona moan, 'Get it, will you, Zoe?' Looking at the clock, Zoe saw it was seven o'clock.

Maggie was already at the front door, her hair dishevelled and her slim figure wrapped in a blue nylon dressing-gown. Zoe padded along the little hallway in time to hear Maggie exclaim, 'George!' in tones of disbelief. Zoe didn't wait to hear any more. She tactfully vanished back into her bedroom, and sat on the edge of her bed, smiling. She heard the door of the sitting-room close and then all was silence again. She stared at the curtains; a delicate lemon light crept through them. It was going to be another miraculous day and she wished she felt more in tune with this glorious summer weather, but her mood was still gloomy and she couldn't even summon the energy to go and make herself some tea. That was probably just as well, of course. She didn't want to disturb Maggie and George, did she?

She slid back into bed and was just lying down again when the door of her room opened softly. Zoe raised her head to gaze through the shadowy dawn light at the figure in the doorway and at first thought her imagination was playing tricks on her. She had to be seeing things. It couldn't be!

'Are you awake, Zoe?' Rory asked softly, and her ears buzzed with hypertension. She wasn't imagining anything. He was here, in her room, and as she stared incredulously he walked over and sat down on the side of her bed.

CHAPTER EIGHT

'How did you get in here?' she asked in a voice that soared, and he leant over and put a hand over her mouth.

'Shssh . . .'

Over the hand her eyes glared and she tried to bite him, but Rory kept her muffled while he murmured, 'I came with George and we wouldn't want to interrupt the love-scene going on in your sitting-room, would we? George is suitably penitent. He's told Lindy and he hopes to persuade Maggie to marry him as soon as they can get it fixed up with the vicar.'

Zoe mumbled furiously and inaudibly.

'Yes, it is good news, isn't it?' Rory agreed blandly, settling himself more comfortably on her bed. His slitted grey eyes surveyed Zoe in a way which made her feel very hot and bothered, suddenly realising that she was only wearing a white silk nightdress which was undoubtedly transparent and which in any case left her shoulders bare and didn't entirely cover her breasts. Rory's wandering gaze infuriated her, and she made a more determined effort to bite the hand silencing her.

'Ouch!' Rory snatched his hand away and looked at the palm in disbelief. 'You vampire! You've left toothmarks and drawn blood!'

'How dare you walk into my bedroom and wake me up!' she threw back, pulling the sheet up to her chin.

'I knew you weren't asleep. I saw you come out of your room and then go back as soon as you realised who was at the front door! Maggie and George didn't notice you, but then they wouldn't have noticed Genghis Khan and all his hordes—they were too wrapped up in each other.' Rory held out his hand. 'Look what you did!'

She looked briefly and saw a faint indentation in his skin; a few tiny marks. 'Where's all the blood?' she sneered.

'Aren't you going to kiss it better?' he asked, eyes mocking, and she gave him a scornful look.

'I won't even bother to answer that!' She clutched her sheet with both hands and said coldly, 'Will you get out of here? I want to get dressed. Go into the kitchen and put the kettle on for some tea. I know how domesticated you are, that shouldn't be too difficult for you.'

Rory didn't move. His eyes had lost their smile and his face was sombre suddenly. 'Why did you bolt like that, Zoe?' he asked in a deep, low voice, and she swallowed with alarm.

'I was only staying with Oliver for a few days. I had to get back to work.'

'You ran away,' Rory said harshly. 'Don't lie about it. You ran away—why?'

Her back to the wall, Zoe couldn't avoid his attack and faced him, trembling slightly and very pale.

'I didn't run. I walked, slowly and deliberately,' she said at last. 'And I wish you'd go now.'

'Are you still angry with me because I didn't explain why I was leaving Provence?' he asked, frowning, his grey eyes searching her face for clues. 'Can't we put that behind us and start again, Zoe? Seven years ago I knew you were the special face I'd been looking for all my life.'

Her heart missed a beat and she bit down on her lip in pain. 'Don't,' she said. 'Please, don't.' She had made her decision and she didn't want him to try to talk her into changing her mind. He had given her all the pain she could take, and she wasn't going to risk getting hurt again.

'It's the truth,' he said huskily, and leaned forward to kiss her, but she hurriedly turned her head away. She couldn't bear it if he kissed her; she couldn't stand any more.

'Go away, Rory,' she stammered, but he took no notice. He was softly kissing her ear and then his mouth began to slide down her throat, warm and gentle and unbearably seductive.

'You know I mean it,' he whispered, and she put a hand up to push his intrusive head away, but it was a bad mistake to touch him, because her fingers loved the feel of that vital dark hair which clung to her skin as if it were drawn by magnetism, little tendrils curling around her fingers, twining around them—or was she involuntarily running her fingers into his hair and letting the strands fall through.

Rory was kissing her bare shoulder, his mouth not missing a single inch of the smooth pale skin, following the bones beneath the skin.

'We've lost seven years,' he said, his mouth pressing down into the warm hollow at the base of her throat. 'But we still have the rest of our lives!'

'No,' she said hoarsely, her face locked in terrified rejection. She couldn't let him hurt her again and he would if she was fool enough to give in to the way she felt.

He lifted his head and looked at her, his restless eyes moving over her. 'Zoe,' he said huskily. 'Oh, Zoe, my God, can't you see how much I want you?'

She shuddered, staring blindly back, struggling not to

get swept away, but her whole body was already caught in a sensual whirlpool which flung her round and round in a dizzying spiral of desire.

With a groan she shut her eyes, her body seemed to be shaking to pieces, she was scared.

She heard Rory's intake of breath, then she was in his arms, her body forced down on the bed by the weight of him, his mouth closing over her lips with an urgency which echoed piercingly inside her. Her arms went round him, her last resistance gone, a moan of anguished pleasure in her throat as his hands caressed her in remembered ways. Every nerve-end knew that touch; her breasts hardened and grew taut under their hot skin, her nipples burning as he stroked them, her body arching up towards his in a spasm of passion.

For a long time after he left her in Provence she had dreamt of this, and now the dream and the reality became a heady explosion in her senses.

She touched him, too; sating the hunger inside her which she had thought cured for ever but which had come back with such force. Button by button she undid his shirt, her hands moving inside it, stroking and caressing while Rory breathed heavily, whispering things that made her tremble.

Once she opened her eyes, briefly, saw his face and was shaken by the feverish colour in his skin, the glitter of his eyes, the tautness of jaw and cheekbone. Their bodies made the sheet she lay on damp with the heat between them as they caressed, and Rory was beginning to take off the rest of his clothes in such a hurry that she heard the rip of material and a smothered swear word from him.

He had taught her to want this pleasure, to need it as

an addict needs his drug, while she was still so young that she had no defences against a man like this or her own feelings, but even as she craved it now the slight interruption gave her time to remember other things—the interminable pain of the months after he had left her, the agony of waking from a dream and finding herself alone. He had left her emotionally crippled, unable to feel anything for any other man, and however hard she tried she couldn't cure herself of wanting him.

She stiffened, putting a hand up to push him away. 'Somebody's coming,' she whispered, hearing movements in the flat.

Rory groaned out a violent comment, his face dark red and sweat glistening on his upper lip. Zoe slid away from him, grabbed up a dressing-gown from the end of the bed and went to the door.

She went out quickly, shutting the door behind her so that Maggie didn't see Rory in the bedroom.

'What's happening?' she asked lightly, and Maggie laughed, her thin face flushed with happiness and her eyes shining.

'George is here,' she told Zoe, who nodded.

'I know. He came with Rory Ormond and Rory told me.'

Maggie looked around, vague and dazed with joy. 'Rory? I didn't see him.' Then she laughed again, even more flushed. 'Oh, yes—of course he was here, I forgot he came with George.' She gave Zoe a helpless little grin. 'I'm a bit light-headed—sorry. Oh, Zoe, I'm walking on air! He's told Lindy and we're getting married right away. I don't know whether I'm on my head or my heels. Thank you, Zoe, I don't know how to thank you.'

'Me?' laughed Zoe, hugging her. 'What did I do?'

'I don't know,' Maggie said, looking surprised and uncertain. 'I've no idea what you did, but until you came to Scarlett we were stuck in a rut and I'm sure George would never have told Lindy. Then you came and everything started to change—it was like an avalanche! One minute everything normal, the next the whole world looks different, and you did it, somehow, although I'm not sure how.'

'I'm very happy for you,' said Zoe. 'I'm sure you and George will be very happy.'

Maggie glowed, nodding silently.

'Why don't you go and get dressed?' said Zoe, laughing. 'And while you're in the bathroom I'll get some breakfast for you and George. He must be hungry, driving all this way. Whatever time did he set out?'

'Apparently he and Rory sat up late last night talking and Rory told him he'd been an idiot, and George said he'd come to London in the morning and Rory said: what's wrong with now? So they just got in a car and took turns at driving. George said he hardly remembers the journey, he was in such a daze, but the roads all seemed quite empty as though it was all a dream, and it only took them just over four hours.'

Zoe paled. 'Good heavens, they must have done a hundred miles an hour all the way!'

Maggie grimaced. 'I know, horrifying, isn't it?' She looked down at herself and groaned. 'Yes, I'd better get dressed, hadn't I? I don't want anything to eat, though, Zoe, I'm not hungry.'

'Coffee will wake you up,' said Zoe, pushing her towards the bathroom, and Maggie went obediently, drifting through the open door as if she really had no idea where she was any more.

Zoe quietly opened her bedroom door. Rory was on his feet and fully dressed by the window. He turned his head to look at her piercingly, the bones of his face almost pushing through his taut skin.

'I'm going to get some coffee and toast for the others. Do you want some?' she asked politely as if they had only just met as total strangers, and his mouth hardened, his grey eyes flashing at her.

'Come here, Zoe. Shut the door.'

She raised her brows. 'Don't bark at me as if this were a parade ground and you were a drill-sergeant!'

'Get rid of George and Maggie as soon as you can, then,' he said curtly. 'We have to talk.'

She gave him a sardonic smile. 'Talking was not what you had in mind just now! And I've decided that what you do have in mind isn't what I want, so when George and Maggie go, you go, too.'

She got out of the room quickly, before he could reach her, but as she shut the door she felt his anger through the panels and shot off down the hall towards the little kitchen, relieved to have escaped and even more relieved to see George hovering uncertainly just inside the sitting-room door.

He went pink when he saw her. 'Oh, hallo, Zoe.'

'Hallo, George,' she said, smiling. 'Congratulations, Maggie told me you plan to get married soon. I'm very glad for you both.'

'Thanks,' he said, moving from one foot to the other, his neck red.

Zoe went into the kitchen and he followed her like a lost sheep, watching her start making coffee as if he had never seen it done before.

'Would you like a cooked breakfast? Egg and bacon?'

She mentally checked the contents of the fridge and hoped she had both egg and bacon. She and Fiona rarely ate a cooked breakfast. A slice of toast was the most they ever bothered with, and it was more often an apple or an orange with some coffee and orange juice.

'If it's no trouble, thanks,' said George. 'I'm starving. I seem to have been awake for a week at least and I could eat a horse!'

Zoe opened the door of the fridge, glanced at the contents, grinned and said, 'Horses we don't have—or bacon, either, I'm afraid, but I could scramble you some eggs and grill you tomatoes and mushrooms.'

He said it sounded wonderful and could he help? She asked him to lay the kitchen table, and he prowled about finding cutlery and cups and saucers while she scrambled his eggs and grilled the vegetables. She was just making toast when Rory walked into the room. Zoe was glad to be able to stand over the stove and pretend that her suddenly heightened colour was due to the heat from the electric hob.

'Oh, Rory!' exclaimed George in blank surprise, as if he had totally forgotten that Rory had come with him, and was wondering what on earth Rory was doing there.

The coffee was percolating violently. Zoe swung to take it off the hob and Rory reached for it at the same time. She snatched her hand away as if the touch of his fingers burnt, and he eyed her in that sidelong, angry way, his eyes narrowed to a steely slit.

'Those eggs are burning,' he told her, and she gave a muffled groan and grabbed for the pan of eggs.

The toast popped up at the same time and a second later she smelt burning from under the grill. Hot-cheeked and confused, she put the pan of eggs down while she rescued the tomatoes and mushrooms.

George discreetly sat down at the table and kept his mouth shut, but Rory laughed, which made her so furious that she almost threw the scrambled eggs at him. She knew she must look an idiot, running from one disaster to another, but it made it no easier to have Rory grinning mockingly at her while she panicked.

She assembled George's breakfast on a plate and put it in front of him. She had done a quick camouflage job on the burnt food; discarding the worst and hiding the rest. George smiled amiably at what was left.

'Thank you, Zoe, it's very kind of you to go to so much trouble for me.'

She smiled back. 'Not at all, a pleasure, George.'

Rory was leaning against the sink, his arms folded and his lean body lounging casually in an attitude which could only be interpreted as deliberate provocation. She knew he hadn't taken his eyes off her since he came into the kitchen and she understood what was going on inside his head. Rory wasn't quite sure why she had suddenly fled again, he was trying to work out her motives, trying to guess what she would do next and no doubt trying to plan a strategy which would outwit her, but Zoe had come very close to the brink of catastrophe a little while ago and she had no intention whatever of allowing him to lure her back towards the edge.

'Coffee?' she asked him coolly after pouring George a cup.

'Thank you,' Rory drawled, watching her fill another cup. 'Don't I get breakfast?' he added softly. 'I drove all night too, you know.'

'Sorry, there are no more eggs,' she said with pleasure,

handing him his cup of coffee. 'Have some toast and marmalade.'

George looked up, a mouth full of egg and a guilty expression on his face. He mumbled something apologetic and Zoe answered firmly, 'Don't be silly, George. Eat your breakfast. He can have muesli if he's really hungry.'

'Thanks, I'd like some muesli,' said Rory, so she had to get it out of the cupboard, which she could only reach by squeezing past him. He made no attempt to move and Zoe made herself very thin to get by without brushing against him. She had to stand on tiptoe to get the muesli box and was constantly aware of his gaze on her body in the thin silk dressing-gown which matched her nightie. Both covered her from neck to toe but neither concealed much. The curve of her body was fully visible and she knew it, fuming as she turned with the muesli in her hand, glaring at Rory as she walked past him again.

He was shamelessly amused by her irritation as he drank some of his coffee and watched her.

'Why don't you sit down?' she snapped, putting his bowl of muesli on the table opposite where George was sitting.

As he moved across the room Fiona wandered in, looking ravishing and sleepily incredulous as she saw the two strange men in the kitchen.

'I thought it was you in the bathroom,' she told Zoe. 'Where did everyone come from?'

Rory's grey eyes held gleaming interest as they wandered over Fiona in her black satin and lace négligé. She hadn't yet brushed her hair and it floated free over her slim shoulders, a delightfully dishevelled blonde cloud, like candy-floss. The fact that she wasn't wearing any make-up at all did nothing to lessen the impact of her looks and Rory's mouth curved in sensual appreciation as he looked at her.

Zoe's stomach sank as if she were in a lift which had suddenly dropped a dozen floors without warning. She knew Fiona and she knew what that look on her face meant—Fiona was assessing Rory with the same narrow-eyed interest. Zoe had long ago learnt to recognise the look on Fiona's face when she saw a man she fancied, and she saw that look now with dismay and a tangle of other feelings she didn't have time to unravel.

'Aren't you going to introduce me?' asked Fiona in her soft, purring voice, her eyes half veiled with pale lids she had lowered to give even more allure to her smile. It was a trick she had. Zoe had never hated it before. It had always amused her, but not now.

'This is Fiona, my flatmate,' she said to anyone who cared to know, not meeting Rory's eyes. She waved a hand at George who put down a slice of toast and half rose, nodding.

'George Ash,' said Zoe, and Fiona ran a glance over him and decided he wasn't worth more than a polite smile.

'Hi.'

'Hallo,' said George, sinking back into his chair and going on with his breakfast as he realised that Fiona had already lost interest in him. She had turned her eyes back to Rory, who watched her with amusement.

'Rory Ormond,' Zoe muttered angrily.

Fiona did a double-take, her eyes opening so wide you could see the perfect whites.

'Rory Ormond?' She looked at Zoe, lips parted on an intake of startled, comprehending breath, and Zoe turned away to pour herself a cup of coffee.

Rory knew at once, of course, that Fiona had heard about Provence. He hid the realisation, though, his face bland and unbetraying.

'So you're Rory Ormond,' Fiona murmured. 'The famous painter, etcetera.'

'Etcetera?' enquired Rory, tongue in cheek.

'I've heard all about you, don't think I haven't,' Fiona told him, and Zoe ground her teeth together. 'I understand now.'

Rory raised his eyebrows. 'What do you understand?'

'Things that were baffling before,' she told him sweetly.

'Your breakfast!' Zoe reminded him in a terse voice, slamming the new toast down on the table. George jumped, looking startled, and Fiona's eyes narrowed on her speculatively, but at that moment Maggie came into the kitchen, distracting everyone.

She had put on a white silk shirt and a grey pleated skirt and looked so happy that if she had been wearing a hairshirt and ashes she would still have looked wonderful. Happiness made her glow like a beacon on a dark night, and Zoe smiled at her.

'The coffee's ready. Would you like some orange juice and toast too?'

George pulled out a chair next to his and Maggie sat down shyly, aware of them all watching her and unused to such attention.

'I'll just have coffee, thanks,' she said huskily.

The kitchen was overcrowded; it was meant to hold two or three people, not a crowd, and Fiona drifted to the door, saying over her shoulder, 'I'll bag the bathroom while it's empty, then.'

Zoe was deeply relieved to see her go but tried not to let that show as she nodded, aware of Rory watching her expression like a cat at a mousehole waiting for the twitch of whiskers.

George looked at his watch. 'We ought to be going soon, Maggie. It's a long drive back. Did you come in your car? We could use that and then Rory could come back in his own car, later.' He gave Rory an apologetic look. 'If that's okay with you, Rory?'

'It's fine by me,' Rory agreed, to Zoe's alarm.

Five minutes later George and Maggie went. Maggie hugged Zoe almost tearfully. 'Will you come up to my wedding? Please try, Zoe. I'd love you to be there.'

'I'll be there,' Zoe promised a little reluctantly. She wanted to go to Maggie's wedding, but she did not want to see Rory again and if she went there was no way she could avoid it.

When they had gone and the front door was closed she glanced at Rory with a stiff little smile, pretending courtesy.

'I have to get ready for work now. I'm sorry, do you mind going? I expect you'll want to be on your way home too.'

As if on cue, Fiona emerged from the bathroom and Rory looked at her smilingly.

'You look gorgeous,' he said, and she did, Zoe had to admit, her teeth tight. Rory didn't have to exaggerate where Fiona was concerned. Whatever she wore she looked stunning, and today she was wearing a chic version of the traditional office uniform—a charcoal skirt, tight and straight, with a waist-trimming narrow black leather belt, and a dazzlingly diaphanous white chiffon blouse with full sleeves ballooning to narrow, tight cuffs. She had swept her blonde hair up on top of her head and pinned it there with a black velvet bow. The swanlike curve of her neck and the demure tilt of her head were contradicted by the wicked glint in her eye as she smiled at Rory.

'Thank you, kind sir,' she cooed, then gave her watch a quick, reluctant look. 'Late again! No time for breakfast, not even coffee . . . damn it! I wish I didn't sleep through my alarm! I'll have to catch a taxi if I can or I'll never get to the city in time.'

'I've got my car outside,' said Rory. 'Can I give you a lift?'

Zoe was icy with fear and anger, but she couldn't move or speak. She stood there and watched them go, knowing she had been afraid of just this from the minute Fiona walked into the kitchen and saw him. Rory didn't even say goodbye. He didn't look at her. Fiona did, briefly, a quick, skating, laughing, defiant look which Zoe returned without expression. She was afraid to show what she was feeling because if she once relaxed her hold on herself she might break into a hundred pieces.

CHAPTER NINE

ZOE hadn't expected to be able to work that morning, but she was in such a hyper state that her head fizzed with ideas, like a bottle of pop after being violently shaken, and when Joe walked into the office she was sharing with several other writers at the agency, he found her alone but oblivious of his arrival as she covered paper with rapid, jerky squiggles. His voice made her jump out of her skin and look round, wild-eyed, at him.

'It's only me, not Jack the Ripper,' he said with amusement. 'You're jumpy today, what's the matter?'

'I'm thinking,' she said, covering the paper with her arm with a secretive movement.

He came closer, peering. 'What's all that? Ideas flowing? Great—fill me in later on our way to the lunch.'

'Lunch?'

'You haven't forgotten?'

Zoe stared blankly, her face admitting she had and he groaned.

'We're lunching with Rudy!'

Horror filled her face. 'Oh, no! Is it today? It can't be!' So much had happened to her since yesterday morning that she had simply expunged Rudy Jamieson from her memory bank and was not very eager to re-admit him.

'It is,' said Joe, laughing at her apalled expression. 'I'll collect you at twelve—we have to be there by twelve-thirty and Rudy won't like it if we're late.'

'Too bad,' Zoe muttered.

'Don't be like that! Remember, we need that contract. And anyway, Rudy's not so bad underneath.'

'Underneath what?' she asked, giving an exaggerated shudder. 'Don't answer, the mind boggles and frankly I've no wish to see underneath. What's on top is quite bad enough.'

'Don't be bitchy,' said Joe, vanishing as suddenly as he had come. It was one of his techniques for keeping an eye on his cohorts—he appeared and disappeared without warning like the Demon King in a pantomime, often catching employees at something they did not want him to know about, like a quiet game of poker in the men's locker-room where they hoped Joe wouldn't think of looking; not that he had any objection to playing poker, but he liked his staff to work during office hours.

Zoe sat for several minutes after he had gone, staring out of the window at the pigeons in their iridescent plumage strutting up and down on a rooftop nearby, the sun striking off their wings and making them as glitteringly exotic as some bird of paradise.

Was Rory on his way back to Cumbria? She hoped so, but her heart misgave her and she bit her lip. She had to hope so! It wouldn't work. He had hurt her too much once before and she was terrified of trying again.

It was some small relief to be sure he couldn't be with Fiona. However wild her leisure hours, Fiona didn't let her fun intrude into her working life—that she took too seriously. She was basically a career-woman; clever and hard-working and clear-headed. She was at her desk from nine until five-thirty, as punctual as clockwork, tackling her paperwork with energy. Fiona's life was compartmentalised, but it seemed to suit her to keep it that way and Zoe couldn't imagine her giving up her career even when she eventually married, as Zoe was sure she would one day. It would be the right man to fit in with Fiona's busy life-style—a man of her own sort, rich enough to support her yet ready to let her continue with her ladder-climbing life at work. Zoe didn't see Rory matching that blueprint. He wouldn't fit with Fiona's smart, sophisticated friends and he wouldn't want to live either in London or one of the stockbroker suburbs.

Fiona might find him amusing for a while, though, and Zoe didn't want to watch them having an affair.

She hoped Rory was on his way back to Cumbria. She hoped she would never see him again.

She wrenched her mind back to her own work and bent her head over the desk again, but the rapid sparkle of ideas had gone flat, she couldn't recapture that first careless rapture. Joe and Rudy Jamieson would have to put up with what she had already come up with, so she gathered up her sheets of paper some half-hour later and shuffled them before she read through to see what exactly she had got.

When Joe came back for her she was just putting the sheets into a handsome folder with the agency logo on the front of it and the name of the account in gold lettering. Joe liked an impressive presentation, even when it was just a rough-out of a possible campaign they were offering to a client. Zoe had often spent weeks trying to come up with something original and then had an idea strike her at the eleventh hour before a vital meeting. At other times you were hit with an idea right at the start and never came up with anything to better it. Advertising was an 'ideas' business and 'ideas' meant people, which meant that it was an expensive business because people cost more than machinery over the year. A good computer could run for years at smaller and smaller costs. A human being of any real originality demanded a high salary and a comfortable office, they were more temperamental than the most contrary of computers, and *they* could be contrary if there was one small flaw in a programme. Zoe knew she was good at her job and she knew Joe was aware of it, too.

He was looking at the folder eagerly, the tip of his nose twitching like antennae.

'Give that to me and I'll read it in the car on the way there.'

She shook her head. 'It isn't fit to read yet. I've put the main points on the top sheet, read that.'

As they went down in the lift he eyed her sideways from head to toe. 'If that outfit was meant to give out a "No" signal to Rudy, it isn't going to work,' he informed her drily.

Zoe had been so absorbed when she dressed that she had forgotten long ago what she had put on that morning and had to look down at herself to check. Only then did she see what Joe meant. Her pleated pink silk dress had the delicate glow of mother-of-pearl; it fell from a square neckline in a smooth unbroken line which gave her figure a grace her more casual clothes never conferred.

'Very classy,' said Joe with satisfaction. 'I'm sure Rudy will approve.'

'Rudy can go . . .'

'Zoe!' he scolded, grinning, as he laid a finger on her lips.

He had an expensive, luxurious car which was no doubt on his expense account, and Zoe was still glowering as she got into it. He skimmed over her notes as they drove to the Mayfair restaurant at which they were meeting Rudy, and she watched him attentively, hoping he liked at least a few of her ideas.

'Promising,' was all he said, though, as he looked up. 'I can see the germ of an idea here and there. We've got plenty of time to kick it around between us, see what materialises out of the scrum.' Joe always used sporting analogies, especially in conference with businessmen who got a point sooner if it was dressed in language they understood.

Zoe had to be satisfied with that. Joe seemed cheerful enough, and, as he said, this was early days yet.

As she followed him into the restaurant's softly lit bar he whispered. 'Now, be nice to him! Remember, he's the *client*.'

Rudy was already there, waiting for them. Zoe felt his pale eyes on her all the way across the room and her teeth met. If only he wouldn't be so obvious about his interest!

'Zoe,' he said, getting up as they reached his table. 'It's been too long since I saw you, this is wonderful.'

She had to give him her hand because Rudy had his own hand outstretched. She knew he would kiss her hand because he always did. Someone, some time, had told him that it made women's head spin to have their hands kissed with Gallic admiration, and Rudy was a bulldog. He never let go of ideas.

'Hallo, Rudy,' she said, carefully not snatching her hand back while Joe watched, although Rudy was taking his time over kissing it and she hoped he wouldn't start eating it any minute.

She wished he wouldn't flutter his eyelashes at her, too. This was one of his flirtatious tricks; Rudy thought it was alluring. Zoe thought it was plain ridiculous, but, retrieving her hand at last, she sat down on the velvet-covered seat next to him and ordered a cocktail from the hovering waiter.

Rudy was a tall, willowy man with light blue eyes and fine, corn-coloured hair. He had a film-star profile; at least, he thought so and used it shamelessly, giving Zoe a view of it while at the same time managing to watch her out of the corner of his eye.

'What have you been up to since we last met?' he asked her and, having given her time to appreciate the beauty of his bone-structure in side view, turned to give her the pleasure of seeing him full face. 'You haven't got married or engaged or anything sinister like that, I hope?'

Wide-eyed and innocent, Zoe shook her head. 'Have you?'

'Me?' he laughed, tossing back his fair head with preening enjoyment of the joke. 'God, no!'

Joe began to edge in talk of the campaign and Zoe quickly asked if she could see a sample of the new products. 'It would be a tremendous help to me at this stage to know what exactly I'm selling.'

'Too early,' Rudy dismissed brusquely. 'We haven't settled on packaging yet. Colours are so vital. Must get them right.'

Zoe had only seen the publicity for the new products given out by Rudy's own people and they had been very vague, merely waffling about a delaying of the ageing process by retaining the natural moisture of the skin, a phrase which she knew to be almost meaningless.

By the time they moved into the restaurant she knew no more than she had when she arrived, and it was clear that Rudy was determined to give away as little as possible. This didn't really surprise her since she knew that industrial espionage was rampant in the cosmetics business and Rudy would fight to the death to make sure no premature hint got out to his rivals.

'It isn't that I don't trust you, Zoe,' he explained as they sat down at their table. 'But we have to be so careful, you know that. This is an important break-through and the most closely guarded secret in our laboratories. It isn't necessary for you to know the formula or any really firm details of the products, is it? You can dream up a campaign which conveys what we want it to convey without giving anything important away!'

'Of course! We understand perfectly,' Joe assured him hurriedly, and Zoe had to agree.

'Yes, point taken, Rudy. We'll carry on with what information we've got and see if we can dream up something for you.'

'I know you can do it, you're so talented and clever,' he said, leaning towards her and taking her hand again, stroking it lightly with one hand while he laid it on the palm of his other hand. 'You amazing girl—you're so beautiful too! That colour was an inspired choice—it gives your skin a ravishing reflection. You have lovely skin, very smooth and clear. Pity you didn't go in for modelling, we could have used you.' He stopped speaking, a frown floating over his face, as someone loomed up behind Zoe. As Rudy lifted his eyes, Zoe glanced round too, and her nerves jumped as she met Rory's eyes. What on earth was he doing here? He couldn't have known where to find her, could he? Had he rung the agency to ask for her and been told which restasurant she was lunching at? No, information like that would never be given out to a stranger.

Zoe's mouth set hard. Fiona! she thought. Fiona knew where I was meeting Rudy. I bet she told Rory—but why would she do that? A movement at Rory's side sent her eyes skating to a newcomer and she took a furious breath as she recognised Fiona in her chic city-wear, a careless and amused smile on her face.

'Hallo, darling,' drawled Fiona, perfection from the sleek blonde hair to the shapely length of her silk-clad legs.

Rudy and Joe stood up, eyes like saucers, and Fiona smiled on them benevolently, accepting their awed reverence as her due.

There was no way Zoe could get out of introducing them and Rudy had no intention of allowing anyone like Fiona to escape without trying to get to know her better. Rory and Zoe stood silent while Rudy arranged it all. Two minutes later they were all sitting at a larger table and Zoe went into an icy silence, but her stiletto eyes warned Fiona that retribution would follow once they were alone, and Fiona's laughing, defiant eyes told her she didn't care.

Fiona had come here to meet Rudy and nothing would have deterred her. The arrival of Rory, as a cover, had been a stroke of luck, but Zoe guessed now that Fiona would have been here whether Rory had turned up or not.

Joe wasn't too pleased, either. His business lunch had turned into something very different and there was no more talk of the campaign. Rudy had other things in mind and other objectives in view. He monopolised Fiona blatantly and she smiled back and dazzled him, playing him far more expertly than he was angling for her, although Rudy didn't seem aware of that.

Joe suddenly remembered Rory's name and leant over to ask, 'Hey, aren't you the painter?'

Rory nodded coolly, and Joe stared as if he had suddenly grown another head.

'I saw your exhibition—loved it. Do you ever do commercial work?'

'All my work is commercial,' Rory told him drily. 'I expect to get highly paid even when I'm painting a landscape for my own enjoyment. I don't see why dealers should get all the money after I'm dead.'

Zoe was staring fixedly at the tablecloth, her face rigid. Joe had been to the exhibition? Then he must have seen the paintings of her. Why hadn't he mentioned it? It wasn't like him to be so tactful.

'Absolutely,' Joe was saying. 'You deserve the reward for your work. Would you be interested in doing some stuff for us? A lot of terrific artists work for agencies now, as you know, and we'd be delighted to have you working for us. On a purely contract basis, of course—a commission for the occasional piece of work, I mean. I've heard you do some wonderful portraits.'

Zoe swallowed, her nerves leaping. How could Joe do this? If he knew, if he had seen those paintings, he must be having a peculiar fun at her expense.

'I rarely do portraits,' Rory said curtly. 'And no, thanks, I don't think I'm interested in your proposition. I'm really too busy at the moment.'

Joe sounded genuinely disappointed. 'Too bad. Some other time, maybe? Keep us in mind if you ever do want to work along that line.'

Rory didn't even promise to do that. He just smiled a little tightly.

'Come to think of it, I didn't see any figure paintings in your exhibition,' added Joe after a little silence. 'Just landscapes and still-life—oh, there was one, a self-portrait. That's how I recognised you. It was damned good, too.'

Zoe looked up, eyes wide and startled, to find herself staring straight into Rory's sardonic face. His mouth took on a mocking curve, but it was Zoe he spoke to.

'I did have some portraits in my exhibition, but I took them out a few days ago.'

Zoe's face washed with a painful colour, her lips trembled and she looked down again at her plate, surprised to see the grilled steak she forgot she had ordered, which she had barely touched. It tasted like sawdust and she gave up the attempt to eat it in the end, hiding it under the lettuce.

The lunch dragged on and Joe became more impatient and irritated by the minute but dared say nothing until they were drinking their coffee when he looked at his watch and said brusquely, 'Well, I'm afraid I've got to rush. Nice to have this talk, Rudy.' That was heavy sarcasm, but Joe half concealed it with a sugary baring of the teeth. Zoe began to get up, too, but he ordered her to stay with a furious, sidelong look. 'Rudy, will you see Zoe gets back to the office? I'm going the other way across town.' He nodded to Rory. 'Good to meet you, Rory, don't forget—any time you feel you'd like to try our game we'd be pleased to hear from you.' He pulled out a card and pressed it into Rory's reluctant hand, threw Fiona a poisoned smile and left, his shoulders angrily hunched.

Rudy looked slightly disconcerted to be left with Zoe on his hands, which was ironic considering he had tried for so long to get her alone, but then he hadn't had a more delectable prospect in view before. He looked from her to Fiona a little ruefully, hesitating.

'I'll get you a taxi, Zoe,' he said at last, but Rory was on his feet too, his manner decisive.

'Leave that to me! I'll get a taxi for her, while I'm paying my share of the bill.'

Rudy protested politely, but Rory refused to let him pay for either his lunch or Fiona's and ended the argument by walking away with Zoe, stopping the head waiter and insisting on being given a bill. Zoe would have escaped at that point, but Rory had seized her arm. It probably looked like a light grip to everyone around them, but she felt the tense curve of his fingers and knew that if she tried to walk away he would tighten that grasp.

When they were outside she turned on him, free to speak plainly now that they were out of earshot of the waiters.

'I'll get my own taxi. Joe was only . . .'

'I'm aware what Joe was trying to do!' he snapped.

'Rudy's a valuable client,' she said, then asked herself furiously why she was explaining to him. What had it got to do with him, anyway?

'Is it part of your job to flirt with the clients, then?' sneered Rory, and her eyes blazed.

'No, it isn't!'

'Then what were you doing when Fiona and I arrived? From where I stood it looked as if you and he were flirting like mad.'

'Rudy always flirts with everyone, it doesn't mean anything.' Rory had begun to walk away, but he hadn't let go of her, he was pulling her along with him, and she tugged at her trapped arm, shaking with impotent rage.

'Oh, Fiona told me all about him,' said Rory, crossing a road in spite of the angry blare of the horn from a passing car. 'She said you disliked him and hated having to meet him, but it didn't look that way to me. You were gazing into his eyes as if he was Sir Lancelot and Robert Redford rolled into one.'

Zoe hissed, 'I was doing nothing of the kind! I was being polite to a client, that's all. It's part of my job—but it isn't part of my job to be polite to you, so unless you want a stand-up fight in the street you'd better let go of my arm!'

She was so intent on her argument with him that she hadn't really noticed where they were going, except to imagine he was walking her back to the office as a taxi hadn't shown up. Suddenly, however, he steered her through swing-doors into the lobby of a Mayfair hotel. She looked wildly around.

'Where are we? What are we doing here?'

Rory put out a hand and pressed the button of the lift. 'I want to show you something, I've got a present for you.'

'Oh, no!' she began in panic, trying to break free.

'You asked me to have those pictures of you taken out of the exhibition, and I did, at once,' he said softly.

She looked up into his face, her eyes dilated, her mouth quivering. 'Yes. Thank you,' she said. 'Why?'

He inclined his head in silence, but as the lift arrived and the doors opened he deftly manoeuvred her into it while she was off guard.

She swung round as she realised as much, trying to reach the panel controlling the lift, but Rory had got there first. The lift began to move upwards and she found him bending towards her.

'This is why,' he said huskily, but she turned her head away before his mouth hit hers.

'Do I have to spell it out for you?' she said in a raw voice. 'I simply don't want to see you. I don't want to get involved with you again.'

Into her hair he whispered, 'Why not, Zoe?'

'Does there have to be a because? Can't you just accept it and leave me alone?'

'No,' he said simply.

It left her speechless and she glanced up at him helplessly. Rory cunningly took his chance to kiss her, his arms going round her as she tried to back away. They swayed together in the lift more as if they were wrestling than kissing. The lift stopped and the doors opened and out of the corner of her eye Zoe saw with flushed dismay a row of three Japanese businessmen gazing at them with great interest.

Rory detached his mouth briefly, looked at the other men, said courteously, 'I beg your pardon. Please take the next lift,' and pressed the button again. The lift doors shut and they went on upwards.

'Oh!' Zoe wailed, feeling like hitting him. 'What on earth must they have thought?'

'I imagine they envied me,' said Rory, grinning shamelessly, then the lift stopped and he urged her out of it and across the corridor to one of the row of white-painted doors.

'I am not coming into your hotel room!' said Zoe, suddenly clear-headed and determined.

'Scared?' he asked, and she gritted her teeth.

'Of you? No, I am not, but . . .'

'Then what's your objection? I'm not planning rape or even seduction—I told you, I have a present for you.'

'I don't want any presents!'

'Not even my pictures of you?'

Her breath caught in her throat, she stared at him in disbelief and he waved a hand through the open door.

'You might as well take them with you now. I'll carry

them down to a taxi for you.'

She walked forward, having seen the canvases stacked in packing cases against a wall. Rory watched her, his face expressionless.

'Want to see them first?'

She shook her head, her throat hot. 'Why?' she whispered when she could speak. 'Why are you giving them to me?'

'All these years they're all I've had of you,' Rory said in a very quiet voice. 'Do you think it was easy for me to walk away like that? I loved you, Zoe. I had to force myself to go and I did it for your sake, but it was the hardest thing I've ever done and each step cost me blood. My head kept telling me it was the right thing to do because if I took you then, when you were so young and didn't really know anything about life or yourself, you might come to hate me later if you ever felt it had been a terrible mistake. I was certain about my own feelings, but how could I possibly bank on yours? If only you hadn't been so damnably young! If I'd had any idea how young you were I'd never have let things go so far, but it was too late by the time I knew. I hated myself afterwards. I knew I might have ruined your life before it really began—don't you think I went through hell? You were the last person in the world I'd have wanted to hurt, and I know it's no use saying that I'm sorry and I never meant it.'

Patiently she asked again, 'But why are you giving the paintings to me now?'

He sighed. 'Because I kept them to remind me of you, they were my only link with you and I hoped in a crazy way that one day they might bring you back to me . . .'

'Is that why you put them in the exhibition?' Her eyes

flashed to his face and saw his mouth twist.

He nodded. 'I hoped you might see them.'

'You set it up?' she realised aloud, her voice startled.

'It was a long shot, but I thought there was a chance as the exhibition was in London. For all I knew you'd married and lived somewhere else, but there was a slim chance and I took it.'

'But if you wanted to get in touch with me why didn't you write to me long ago?'

'I had no idea where you lived,' Rory said impatiently. 'We never exchanged that sort of information, did we? I knew your family were from London, but my God, Zoe, how many Strouds do you think there are in the London telephone directory? I didn't even know which suburb you came from. And I couldn't ask the people at the hotel. My name was mud in that direction. They wouldn't have told me, and anyway, seven years ago I thought I was saying goodbye to you for ever. I didn't dare think ahead. I ran and tried to forget you, but I couldn't. Every time I saw your face in my paintings I got the same stab of feeling, it never altered through the years. You may have lived away from me, Zoe, but for seven years you've been living with me day in, day out, and now that I've seen you again I know I can't go on like that any longer. I'll go crazy if I do. Either I have you or I end it here and now. That's why I'm giving you the paintings. Take them or take me with them, but I couldn't stand the sight of them any more. Hope deferred maketh the heart sick, and I've lived on the hope of seeing you for seven years, my darling.'

She closed her eyes, her face pale and her body weak, and Rory took a step nearer but didn't touch her. She heard him breathing next to her and bit down on her lip, torn between love and fear.

'Rory, give me time to think this out,' she said huskily at last. 'I don't know what to do. I told myself I couldn't risk caring for you again, but that wasn't true because I never stopped, but . . .'

'Zoe,' he broke in, his voice shaking. 'Zoe darling, I love you so much. Don't go away again, I can't bear it.'

'Don't pressure me, Rory!' she cried out, a hand flung up to halt him as he moved closer.

'You love me,' he said, and although he pretended it was a question it was a statement. Rory knew she loved him; she had always loved him. There could never have been anyone else, and it wasn't only fear that had stopped her falling in love again, she had always lied to herself about that because it was humiliating to admit she still loved a man who had walked out on her without looking back.

'I can't think with you near me,' she moaned, and he laughed softly, moving even closer. Her lifted hand was no barrier. He kissed it; his lips hot against her palm.

'I need you,' he said, taking hold of the hand and laying it against his cheek. Her fingers strayed of their own accord and felt the hard bone structure under his warm flesh, felt the pulse leap up in his neck as she touched it. Rory might lie to her, but his body couldn't lie, and she felt his heartbeat thundering as he took her in his arms, felt him tremble as his mouth hunted for hers, felt his fingers shake as they closed around her waist and drew her closer.

'The minute I saw you again I knew you were still mine,' Rory told her, his voice exulting, and she tried to whip up anger against him for being so sure of himself, but all her anger seemed to have seeped away and she

knew that she had felt, too, that the invisible bond
between them still existed. The minute she saw him
again she had wanted him as passionately and intensely
as ever, and if she was honest with herself she had known
that Rory wanted her too.

'Don't be afraid, Zoe,' he whispered as his mouth
tenderly moved against hers. 'I've got you,' he said, as he
might one day say to a child of theirs who was afraid of
falling and who would nestle as gratefully as she did into
his strong, sure arms.

She couldn't hold back the feeling any longer; it flared
up in her as strongly as ever and she was fire and silk in
his arms, she was flying, beyond the touch of fear and
pain, and if it was only for this instant that didn't seem to
matter because their love had already stood the test of
time and long, bitter separation. Nothing could hurt
either of them now, except the loss of each other.

Can you keep a secret?

You can keep this one
plus 4 free novels

COMING NEXT MONTH

1087 MY BROTHER'S KEEPER Emma Goldrick
Mickey is over the moon to have Harry home again. Life is good with her
stepbrother around. Yet it's strange that she finds her thoughts
centering less on her fiancé, George, and more on Harry....

1088 JENNY'S TURN Vanessa Grant
Making award-winning documentaries with Jake has been fun! However,
when he declares his intention to marry her best friend, Jenny decides to
leave. She'll never be one of Jake's women, but she can't stand the
thought of him marrying someone else!

1089 FIGHT FOR LOVE Penny Jordan
When Natasha makes friends with an old Texas rancher in London, she
never dreams that one day he'll leave her a legacy in his will. It isn't until
she's at his ranch near Dallas that she begins to guess at his motives.

1090 FRAZER'S LAW Madeleine Ker
Rio enjoys studying the marine life off Australia's untamed Cape York
Peninsula. She resents the intrusion of biologist Cameron Frazer into her
remote solitude. But having to fight danger together makes her realize
just how much they have in common.

1091 WHEN LOVERS MEET Flora Kidd
Jilly couldn't say that Ed Forster hadn't warned her. He'd made it very
clear from the start that he wasn't interested in commitment. Recently
widowed Jilly, however, isn't ready for a "torrid tropical affair"!

1092 NO MAN'S MISTRESS Roberta Leigh
A woman would have to be a real man-hater not to appreciate
Benedict Peters—and Sara is no man-hater. Just the same she isn't going
to join the admiring throng that sits at his feet—no matter how
persuasive he is!

1093 REASONS OF THE HEART Susan Napier
Meeting Ross Tarrant brings Francesca's adolescent humiliation back
with a jolt. Older and wiser now, successful in her way of life—surely she'll
have the upper hand over the seemingly lackadaisical Ross. It just doesn't
work out that way, though.

1094 DISHONOURABLE INTENTIONS Sally Wentworth
Rex Kynaston has everything it takes to attract a woman. The trouble is,
he knows it. Not that it matters to Harriet. As far as she's concerned, he's
the last man on earth she'd get involved with....

Available in July wherever paperback books are sold, or through
Harlequin Reader Service:

In the U.S.
901 Fuhrmann Blvd.
P.O. Box 1397
Buffalo, N.Y. 14240-1397

In Canada
P.O. Box 603
Fort Erie, Ontario
L2A 5X3